P9-APH-339

Back to Before

1C
L275
a

Back to Before

JAN SLEPIAN

Philomel Books   New York

Copyright © 1993 by Jan Slepian
Published by Philomel Books,
a division of The Putnam & Grosset Group,
200 Madison Avenue, New York, NY 10016.
All rights reserved. This book, or parts thereof,
may not be reproduced in any form without
permission in writing from the publisher.
Published simultaneously in Canada.
Book design by Patrick Collins
The text is set in Garamond Simoncini.

Library of Congress Cataloging-in-Publication Data
Slepian, Jan. Back to before / Jan Slepian. p. cm.
Summary: Eleven-year-old cousins Linny and Hilary find themselves
transported back to their old Brooklyn neighborhood to a time just
before Linny's mother died and Hilary's father left home.
[1. Space and time—Fiction. 2. Mothers and sons—Fiction. 3. Fathers and
daughters—Fiction. 4. Cousins—Fiction. 5. Death—Fiction.] I. Title.
PZ7.S6318Bac 1993 [Fic]—dc20 92-10103 CIP AC
ISBN 0-399-22011-9

10 9 8 7 6 5 4 3 2 1

First Impression

For Kaia in my heart,
and her father, Christopher.

Chapter 1

Lionel Erda, almost twelve and slightly crazy (as he would be the first to say), gave his order to the waitress at the bus depot in Albany. The ghost who lived inside his head said, "Linny, that's junk food!"

"And a cherry Coke," Linny mumbled, as much to the ghost as to the waitress.

"Whadja say, kid?" The waitress tapped the pencil on her pad, letting him know she didn't have all day.

Thwip! Off went her head, skimming across the room like a Frisbee.

As he munched his chili dog he looked to see who was next.

At the far end of the counter he spotted Pigface, whom he had wanted to kill on the ride up. Linny glared at him. With that nose you could see up to his brains. The kid had started in with him soon after they boarded the bus at the Port Authority in New York City.

At first Linny had tried to ignore the rhythmic kicks on

the back of his seat, the spitballs that landed on the back of his head, the bubble-gum breath in his ear. Finally he had turned around and said, "Do you mind?" He cringed at the memory. Do you mind! he mocked himself. He wanted to sound like King Kong and instead was Mickey Mouse. Pigface had just grinned at him.

For that moment alone, the kid had to die. Linny unleashed his beam and off went the head, rolling away on twelve white tiles and eleven black ones. He had counted them as he walked to the counter. When the waitress wasn't looking he had arranged the silverware in a straight line. He had managed to sit down on the stool from the left side, not the right. So far he had managed to do what he had to do without attracting attention.

He wouldn't have been able to explain to a living soul why in the past year he needed to do these fool things only in a certain way. He only knew that these counting and listing and arranging routines made him feel safer. They made him feel as if he had some control over what he had learned was a very chancy existence.

He observed the man sitting next to Pigface. The father, Linny supposed. He had to go too. He had gone on sleeping while his cretin son was tormenting innocent people. *Thwip.*

Linny swallowed hard, trying to put a lid on the rage that seemed to well up out of nowhere.

"A mess," he had heard his father tell Aunt Helen the night before on the phone, and he wasn't talking about his sock drawer. He had said it in a hoarse whisper, but Linny heard. He was wide awake in that lumpy bed and heard it all.

2

"He can't even sit down straight anymore without some extra footwork. I tell you, Helen, I got to get myself an office job with regular hours so I can have him with me again. I can't keep on doing this traveling. It's killing me. My parents mean well, but this isn't working out."

He saw his father's face in his mind's eye and felt again the shock of how suddenly old he looked. It happened that instant when Linny had gotten off the plane in New York two days before and glimpsed his father waiting for him behind the barrier. It had been only a few months since he'd seen him, but at first sight this man was different, changed. It had lasted only a breath, but Linny saw him as a stranger would. The next instant the strangeness had dissolved and there was his father again, his smile sad, his hair sparser and his eyes anxious. His hug and smell were so familiar, so full of all that was over and done with that Linny could hardly stand to be close to him.

These last two days, before boarding the bus, Linny had been with him back in Brooklyn, not in his old house, but in a rented room near the park, with brown wallpaper and a bathroom down the hall. His father stayed at that rooming house now when he wasn't driving from one town to another down South with his sample case in the backseat.

What was it he used to call himself, and everyone would laugh? Linny could never see the joke.

"What joke?" said the ghost in his head. "There's nothing funny about a 'traveling salesman'! Believe me, I know. He's never home."

An image of his old Brooklyn neighborhood rose unbidden in Linny's mind, like a snapshot placed before him. He saw the trees along the curb, the red brick of the houses lining the quiet street. He saw his younger self look up to the apartment that used to be his home. His mother was sitting at the window, leaning out, watching the street because it was one of her good days.

He blinked and squashed that. Mashed it, stepped on it and threw it away.

The bus driver called an end to the lunch stop. From Albany to Colchester, Vermont, his destination, Linny leaned his forehead on the cool glass and watched the scenery go by. Behind him, Pigface was slumped against his father, mercifully asleep.

Linny thought of what he had left behind in Pittsburgh, where he had lived with his grandparents for the past year, and he could have kicked himself. His beloved computer he couldn't bring. No way. But why had he left his skateboard behind? There were no sidewalks or skatepark at the barn, but at least he could have looked at it every night. He missed it already.

Linny let that go and concentrated. He cut off all the telephone poles at the root as the bus sped by. *Thwip, thwip,* let 'em all drop. For good measure he did away with the trees.

Hilary sat on the bench next to her mother, waiting for her cousin Linny's bus to arrive in the Grand Union parking lot. She hummed to herself in order to blot out the conversation next to her.

Her mother was always meeting people she knew as a girl, having been raised and gone to school in these parts. Today it was Mrs. Fried-egg, whom her mother had recognized sitting on the depot bench in the parking lot. Fried-egg couldn't be the name of an actual person, but Hilary's attention had been more on the perfect roll of fat under the broad face than on the introduction. Like wearing a glazed doughnut around your neck, she thought. It seemed impossible to her that this puffy old thing had been at school with her mother. Granted that Hilly couldn't stand her mother, she had to admit she was pretty—in a disgusting female way.

Fried-egg had given the big, clumsy daughter of her old school chum a hard look, and Hilary at once supplied the inner thoughts that went with it. The girl is a linebacker if I ever saw one, Hilly imagined the woman saying to herself. And dressing like one doesn't help, wearing those old running shorts, and golf cleats on those big feet, of all things. That hair needs to be tamed with a whip. The poor girl didn't inherit her mother's looks, that's for sure.

Hilary noticed the woman examining her mother's face with curiosity. Again she could almost hear her say, Hmmmm, still pretty, I see, but I hear there's trouble at home.

A small, satisfied smile curled the lips of Fried-egg. "My, she's a tall one," she said. "How old are you, sweetheart?"

"Forty-three," replied Hilary serenely.

Her mother flushed with a combination of annoyance and suppressed amusement. She hated any hint of lying or even exaggeration in her daughter, as if it were an inherited disease handed down by Hilary's father. Yet a laugh was grudgingly pulled from her at Hilary's silliness.

This made her bench companion purse her lips in

disapproval. Fresh mouths should be punished, the heavy face declared.

"Pay no attention to my ridiculous child. She's only eleven. Can you believe it? She was always tall for her age. I believe she's the only child on this planet who was taller than her own kindergarten teacher. But tell me about yourself, Hazel. You still live near Pike's Falls?"

Without waiting for an answer she plunged on. "Remember we used to go to Pike's after school, daring one another to go skinny-dipping in broad daylight? Whatever became of Charlie Cunningham, Hazel? He caught us that one time and we screamed so, we near scared him to death. Remember? Never mind about him, tell me about yourself. You happy?"

Her companion's eyes had begun to glaze over in her attempt to follow this conversation. The red mouth opened and closed like a fish out of water.

Hilary recognized the signs and smiled grimly to herself. Her mother specialized in the roller-coaster effect. You had to hang on to the subject for dear life. Instant intimacy was the result if you could stay with it.

Fried-egg, you haven't heard anything yet, Hilary thought. She's going to talk to you about my father in a minute, I just know it. Don't think you're special, she said to the visitor soundlessly. My mother would talk to bed-bugs if there were no one else.

It was a hot August day in Vermont. Hilary flapped the neck of her T-shirt to stir up the air a bit. She stood to peer up the street in the direction the bus would come from. Traffic was heavy and the cars were bumper to bumper, inching along the narrow, sun-drenched street. No bus in sight.

She left the bench and prowled along the sidewalk in front of it, enjoying the clickety-click of her spikes on the pavement. The town was crowded with shoppers going from one discount store to another. Hilary walked among the streams of people and looked about like a stranger.

Colchester had changed in her short lifetime from a quiet town to one big outdoor shopping mall. She had spent every summer of her life at the barn, and the half-hour trip down the mountain to town used to be a big treat. She remembered going to it with her father on one of his rare weekend visits. She was his shadow then, not wanting to let him out of her sight. If she was patient while he swapped jokes and had a few at the Klondike bar, he would take her afterward to Mother Macree, the best-smelling store in the world. She could have any ice cream she wanted—never mind that her mother was a health nut almost as bad as Aunt Josie.

Like her aunt used to be, she amended.

Now Mother Macree was a boutique and her father lived far away. Why should he stay with a wife who didn't appreciate him?

At last. She saw the New York bus trundle down the street, heading for its reserved space in the supermarket parking lot.

Her mother was still deep in conversation and didn't notice the arrival of the bus. Hilary hung back from the descending passengers, suddenly shy about meeting her cousin after looking forward to it so much. Would he be changed, she wondered.

She hadn't seen him since he went to live with his grandparents in Pittsburgh a whole year before. No longer did he live around the corner from her in Brooklyn. They used to practically live in one another's house.

She shaded her eyes from the sun and saw the dark skinny boy step down from the bus. He was wearing a white short-sleeved shirt tucked into pressed tan chino pants.

He's gotten neat, she noted with a tinge of dismay. He also had a new funny hunch to his narrow shoulders. It made him look smaller than she had expected, instead of bigger. He still had the glossy black curls that she would have gladly exchanged for her own wild frizz, and he also had the same quietness about him.

She had to grin at the sight of him standing there, waiting patiently for the driver to dig out his suitcase from the belly of the bus. It was so typical of him. She would have been galoomphing around like an elephant, tripping over her own feet, searching the crowd, not caring if people stared. He just stood there, neat, calm, contained as a grandpa.

Hilary ran back to her mother, who was still absorbed in her conversation. "He's here! Come on!"

"Why didn't you tell me! Say good-bye to Mrs. Freedeck, baby. Come see me, Hazel. You remember our old barn."

"Sure do. Sorry about your trouble, Helen," said Hazel Freedeck, who clearly wasn't sorry at all.

Aside from "Hi, shrimpo," Linny didn't say one word

to Hilary. She wanted to pick him up and swing him around in a hug, she was that glad to see him. But something about him stopped her. Had he even smiled? As she hung back she noticed he stayed in her mother's embrace longer than for just hello but then stepped back in a hurry.

Hilary turned away in disgust at the tears running down the sides of her mother's nose. She picked up Linny's bag and carried it to their van which had been parked in the hot sun near the supermarket entrance. She thought of her cousin's closed face. Something was gone from it. Some lift or light that once was there and now was not.

They had always been close, but now they had something in common they had never had before. They both were without, without what they needed, like a couple of homeless. His mother had died, and her father sent postcards.

Chapter 2

Linny didn't notice the sidelong glances of his Aunt Helen as they drove up the mountain. The van was filled with her voice, but he didn't feel like talking just yet. Later he'd talk, first let him be, first let him soak up the ever-rising road, the thick bordering trees, the outline of the mountains rolling off in the distance. Soon they would come to Indian Rock, then the half-painted house, the dump road and then the turn, the weedy path, the rickety barn. These were all landmarks he had searched for in dreams of returning to the one solid place left to him, the summer place of all his childhood.

He knew his aunt was speaking, but in the past year he had discovered how to go away whenever he wanted. He could just turn himself off, like pressing the mute button on a TV. He didn't notice her quick silent exchange with Hilary behind him in the backseat: lifted shoulders, rolled eyes, downward mouth, all meaning, Hey, what is this?

They came to the half-painted house, half yellow, the

other half left a weathered gray, as if the owner had either run out of money or had a change of mind. As they drove past, Hilary leaned over to shove her palm in front of her cousin for him to slap. This had always been their ritual at this landmark. It meant they were almost to the barn, almost home. Linny startled as the hand appeared, and he stared at it for an instant as if he had never seen one of those things before. Then he seemed to recollect what he should do. His hand lifted and slapped hers in the old way.

Suddenly the windshield in front of them darkened as if the sun had fallen out of the sky. At the same time, or so it seemed, something gave the van a terrible blow from above and the windshield exploded, showering Linny and his aunt with glass.

The van swerved sideways from the impact and stalled in the middle of the road. It all happened so fast no one had time to react. No one screamed or even moved. They sat for a moment without a word, just breathing in and out.

Aunt Helen spoke first. "Anybody hurt?" She was staring straight ahead, too shocked to take it all in. She lifted a limp hand and began brushing off splinters of glass as if they were so much harmless confetti. One of the slivers jabbed her and she came to life crying, "What happened! Hilary, are you all right! Linny! Don't anyone touch the glass!" She was shaking now.

"Mom?" said Hilary in a small voice.

Linny groaned. It was the queerest thing. At the big knock, he felt as if he had split into two people. One of him was having the accident, and the other self was float-

11

ing a little above, watching it happen, like a bystander. The tremendous blow, the explosion, the swerve of the van, the danger they were in didn't scare him a bit while it was going on.

Now it was a different story. It was over. He was one person again but felt as if he had just lost every bone in his body. His arms and legs felt like spaghetti.

A man stuck his shaggy blond head through the driver's window. "Helen!" he cried. "Are you okay?"

"What? Oh, Taylor! What are you doing here? I think so. We hit something. No, I think something hit us."

"Yup, look there." He pointed across the road, where a large doe lay heaving on the grassy shoulder. "From the looks of the windshield I'd say she was trying to leap it and didn't make it. Shame, the deer is a goner, but I thank almighty God you all are okay. Hilary? Hi, young feller. You people could have been killed, accident like that."

"Oh, no!" cried Hilary. "A deer? Is it dead? I'm going to go see." She fumbled with the door, but she was still too shaky to get it open.

Taylor said, "We were just two cars back. When I saw it was you Helen, why . . ." He stopped and shook his head as if nothing he said could do justice to that moment.

He straightened and slapped the side door. "Come on, everybody out. Let's get this car off the road. Walt?" He yelled to a boy near the fallen deer. "Come help push. We need to let these folks by." He motioned to the cars lined up behind them. There were a few backed up by now, waiting to get through. Some others had parked and the occupants were standing around the deer.

A boy about Linny's age, a smaller edition of Taylor

Dilt, with the same long bony face but more yellow-haired, helped push the damaged van to the side of the road.

Both the man and the boy were new to Linny. He didn't like his aunt and cousin having new friends, people he didn't know. He had wanted everything to remain exactly the same.

It was clear that Hilary didn't like them either. Linny saw her brush by them without a glance or a thank you. That was odd, since she was always falling for people, making them more than what they were.

Linny and Hilary crossed the road and stood by the stricken deer, and looked at it in silence. The animal struggled to rise, then sank down. Its eyes opened, rolled in terror and closed. It lay on its side, slick and heaving, ringed by people watching its throes at a respectful distance. Death was in the air, stilling talk, finding inside every onlooker the place it owns. Second by second it took away the light of the fallen creature.

Linny was fighting anger and a surge of tears which bewildered him since crying didn't come easy to him. Not even about his own mother. How come now, over some animal?

Across the way, a child giggled nervously. Linny unleashed his beam to send the offending head to the trees.

Next to him Hilary moaned, half to herself, "Ooh, if only . . ."

Linny continued her thought but to himself. One little minute, he said to himself. I could have stopped to tie my shoe. The bus could have been late. He was filled with regret, filled with wanting to go back and change things.

If only time didn't work just one way, they could go back. He would stop to take a drink and delay by minutes getting into the van. If he had, the beautiful deer would be unharmed, and bounding through the woods that very minute. If only he could go back and undo what had happened!

A policeman and vet arrived at that moment, and when Linny and Hilary saw the vet's gun they fled back to the van.

When the tow truck came, Taylor Dilt gave them a ride to the barn in his pickup. Aunt Helen sat up front with him.

In the open back Hilary and Linny sat leaning against the cab, the wind whipping their hair. Walt sat against the side and didn't seem to notice or care that he was being ignored. He was leaning on a tarp-covered mound of something large. It had the shape of a thick tree trunk.

"What's that?" yelled Hilary, the wind grabbing her words. It was the first time she spoke to the Dilt boy.

Walt cupped a hand behind his ear.

Hilary pointed to the covered mound and asked the question with her palms and raised eyebrows.

"Something my dad works on," said the boy, turning amiable gray eyes to her. He was neither friendly nor unfriendly and surely not talkative. That was all he volunteered.

Hilary spoke into Linny's ear so Walt wouldn't hear. "See? You can't get anything from him. They bought the old Needham house. You know? The one by the river. Just him and his dad. He's a carpenter, his father. Comes over a lot. I can't stand him or his son. Borrring!"

Linny nodded and kept his eyes on the backward view, wondering if it was better to face front and see what was coming, or to look back at where you had been.

Hilary poured into his ear. "They used to live around our way. In Brooklyn, I mean. Ever see him?"

Linny looked at the unconcerned boy, looked back at the receding road and shook his head no.

"Mom told his father about this place. Told him about Colchester, I mean. Taylor'd been working on the Sternlieb house back home, and he and Mom got to talking, surprise, surprise. You know how she is. He said he was looking to move up north and she told him about the Needham place. That was so dumb! That Walt is a creep, don't you think? Always coming around, not saying anything. Who does he think he is?"

Linny didn't venture a guess, since the pickup had stopped. They were at the barn.

As they climbed out, Taylor walked Helen to the door. He said something to her. She glanced quickly at her daughter and then shook her head no.

Taylor returned to his truck and he and Walt drove off, the boy waving a careless so long.

Linny picked up his suitcase and walked to the big double door as slowly as he could bear to. This was the best, this time just before actually entering the barn.

He stood on the threshold, letting himself get accustomed to the dimness after the glare of the sun. He breathed in the mixture of dust and age and flowers and what he swore was cow dung even though the barn hadn't seen a cow for generations.

When he was little, his mother had told him that what

tickled his nose in that doorway was fairy dust. He thought that was silly even then, but the words jumped to his mind whenever he thought of the barn.

He had once tried to describe the place to his friend Eddie Gilberto, and when he was done Eddie had said, "It sounds like a dump!" He had never felt the same about Eddie since.

Linny had told him about the enormous papier-mâché bird flying over the fireplace, the swing hanging from the rafters, the snow shoes on the wall, the prodigal fling of couches and chairs and old rag rugs. He had tried to describe the color and jumble and joy of the place. Then he quit talking about it because he just didn't have the words. Like going to Oz, Hilary once said, in the faraway days when she approved of her mother.

It always surprised him that such a place could have come from his Aunt Helen. She always seemed to him as practical and down-to-earth as a building beaver, always in motion, always busy, always talking, talking.

Again the ghost spoke. "My sister Helen has a streak of romance in her a mile wide. She sits on it because of that worthless husband of hers. He has enough foolery in him for both."

Linny didn't know if he was remembering a conversation or making it up. He had no idea what the voice meant about his Uncle Hal. Hilary's father was a lot of fun when he was around. Especially when he was drunk. All Linny knew for sure was that it was his mother speaking loud and clear in his head, as plainspoken and direct as always. A sure sign that he was going crazy.

He walked about the barn slowly and silently to say

hello to old friends: the line of funny old hats hung on a beam under the loft, the wheezing old pump organ in the corner, the fireplace stone where he used to leave notes for his mother to find. The family bike leaned against the far door as usual. Nothing was changed, everything was changed.

He climbed the wall ladder to the loft and unpacked his things, hanging what he could on the nails and leaving the rest in neat piles on the cot next to his bed. He put on his bathing suit and plunged down the raspberry path to the shallow brook, with Hilary loping after him. He was in a fever to see what had happened to the dam they had made when he was last there the year before.

The water was low for August, barely covering the rocks in the brook. The boulders they had once piled to form a small pool were now scattered helter-skelter, the tops exposed and dried in the sun like old gray bones.

Linny waded in and began to rebuild.

Nearby, Hilary stretched out belly-down on the sunning rock, a flat slab anchored to the middle of the narrow brook. She absently scraped the bottom, bringing up a handful of pebbles to examine and then discard. She had been waiting for this time when they were alone. Now they could talk.

She sat up suddenly, holding up one of the pebbles in her hand. It was a round white stone, perfectly shaped. "Hey! Linny, look what I found! A magic pebble!"

Linny looked up briefly. "Oh yeah, sure." He had outgrown nonsense.

He had been piling the stones one on top of another to dam the water. Now he began to fling them down, making

17

them bounce off one another with a loud crack, making them splash. For some reason he needed to do that.

"Quit that! Look what you did!" Hilary was wet. "What's the matter with you? What are you so mad at?"

"Sorry about that. I'm not mad." What was he going to tell her? He was mad at some rocks? That's what it felt like.

"Well, I'm saving this pebble to give to my dad."

Linny knew Hilary's father was someplace in L.A. He had overheard talk that even before the divorce was final, his Uncle Hal was out there with another woman. How much Hilary knew about this he had no idea. It had all happened the past year, when Linny was in Pittsburgh, a lifetime away from when the two families were close.

He straightened and, for the first time since he arrived, focused on his cousin. He looked at her directly and said, "What do you mean, you're giving that to your father? I heard that after your mom threw him out he went to L.A. You going out there?"

"Maybe I am! And what do you mean, my mom threw him out? Never! Never in a million years. He's the one. He left her!" She stood tall and outraged on the rock, shouting at him. "It's all her fault!" she yelled.

"Okay, okay," he said, continuing work on the dam. Hilary could never see straight when it came to her father. He could do no wrong. "A daddy's girl," agreed the ghost, his mother, in Linny's head.

As he thought about his Aunt Helen he remembered how Taylor Dilt, that man who had helped them out that afternoon, had looked at her. There was something between them. Linny didn't dare mention it to Hilary.

But that night he was awakened by something, a noise, a moan, like someone crying. At first he thought it was the ghost, weeping the way he would find her sometimes on her sofa when he came home from school. And as always when he thought of her, guilt and grief roared through him like wind.

But then he realized this noise came from outside himself, from someplace downstairs.

He raised himself on his elbows and peered over the edge of the loft. Below the giant flying bird, silhouetted against the flames in the fireplace, were Taylor Dilt and his Aunt Helen in an embrace. It was Taylor who was crying.

Chapter 3

➤ Hilary found the whole thing ridiculous. "Taylor crying?" Her laugh echoed in the vacant, decaying room. "Taylor Dilt, Mr. Personality himself? That stick? You must have been dreaming."

They had bicycled down the dump road early that morning, under an unfriendly sky, to explore the abandoned house Hilary had discovered the day before Linny's arrival. The dirt road they took was completely familiar, but neither of them had ever noticed the cottage before.

The day of her discovery, Hilary had plunged into the thickets that bordered the road to get to the brook she could hear but not see. It was part of the Battenkill, the same stream that meandered behind the barn. She was out collecting mushrooms, a new interest, and hoped to find some chanterelles growing on the banks. It was late in the season for them, but she might get lucky. And there, hidden from the road, quite near the water, was a falling-down cottage, abandoned and rotting.

The door was off its hinges, the doorway gaping. Hilary had peered in. Very spooky. Images of corpses lying around in there, faces eaten by rats, crowded her imagination. It was late and she had to go. She would bring Linny when he came. It was just the place to explore with him.

But now that he was here, Linny had more on his mind than the old house. He and Hilary were stepping gingerly through the rotting rooms, trying not to put a foot through the flimsy boards, when he told her of the scene between his Aunt Helen and Taylor Dilt the night before.

Hilary was intent on showing him how mistaken he was to think there might be something going between her mother and Taylor Dilt. It just couldn't be.

There was no place to sit in that tilted and junk-strewn room, so she faced him near what was once a sofa and ticked off her points on her fingers. "First of all, I already told my mother that I can't stand him, he's so boring. I mean, she knows how I feel. She even agreed with me. I mean, she said not to worry my head, he wouldn't be coming around much."

Another point, another finger. "Second, forget the romance. Maybe if there were only two females left in the world and the other was a camel, maybe she could get a man. And that's only a maybe. She couldn't keep my father, could she?"

At the mention of her father Hilary began to prowl around, tripping over the debris on the floor, circling Linny. Talk about her father spilled out of her as if a plug had been pulled. She was making no sense at all. "After him, how could she go for anyone else? She says he lies. Well, it's not lies just because he forgets. I mean, so what if once in a while he stayed out? Maybe if she didn't complain so much. . . . She just didn't know him. Take his drinking, for instance. Or that time with the Ice Capades? I didn't mind, honest. He explained it all to me. I mean, he's going to send for me. We're going to live together. He said so on a postcard. I miss him so much! Someone like my daddy wouldn't . . ." There was so much that her daddy wouldn't, she gave up. Defiant tears welled up.

Linny listened to her ramble and for the first time since his arrival saw his cousin's pain and confusion. He heard her find excuses for her father, heard her protecting herself from doubts, as if she were putting a bandage on an open wound.

"So," Hilary finished lamely, "that's stupid about her and Taylor Dilt."

She rested a foot on the broken-down sofa, and her round, hopeful face looked down and away to avoid what she saw in Linny's knowing eyes.

She noticed something near her shoe. "Hey, what's that?" She kicked away the mouse droppings in the exposed stuffing of the sofa. What fell to the floor was a ring.

Hilary and Linny reached for it at the same time and hung on to it as if it were a wishbone they were sharing. It turned into a game they both wanted to win. They pulled back and forth, back and forth, for possession of the ring. Finally, by sheer weight, Hilary managed to yank it away from him.

She held it up to a window that let in some outside light. The ring, a dull copper almost black with age, was a plain circlet, too large for a finger and too small for a bracelet.

They couldn't see it plainly; the room was too dim. The house was surrounded by overgrown bushes and trees, which shut out what little light might have penetrated the growth. It was gloomy inside, clammy and chill, and smelled of rust and mildew. The ring couldn't be seen clearly enough.

They took it outside, and standing near the collapsed porch, Hilary rubbed it between her fingers. She saw a gleam.

"Gold!" she cried rapturously, looking at Linny with big eyes. "This is the most amazing thing! What is it? I knew we would find something special here!"

"Go on," said Linny, her whimsy an irritation to him. "Here, let me see." He turned it over, examined it, rubbed it some more and shook his head at Hilary, pitying such foolishness. "Know what this is? It's a shower curtain ring! Gold," he said derisively. "What planet do you live on?" The anger was rising in him suddenly.

"Oh, you!" She grabbed it from him. She walked a few steps away and then whirled at him. "What's the matter with you, anyway? Ever since you came it's like you're the smart one. You know everything, right? Look at you, your eyes do that funny blink and you act like you're a hundred years old. Well, Mr. Smarty, if you know so much, show me where there's a shower in this house."

This wiped the mockery from Linny's face. There was no shower in the one and only bathroom! He had seen an old chipped tub on its side, but no shower fixture. Still . . .

"Here, let me see it again." He rubbed off more of the black from the ring and nodded to himself. "Okay, maybe it's not from a shower curtain, maybe they used to have drapes here. Whatever, it's nothing. Brass, I think, or maybe steel. Something like that. Definitely not gold. Only a kid would think that."

He was about to hand it back to her, when something prompted him to pocket it. He wanted it. "I'll clean it up, okay?"

"No, I'll do it. It's mine!" said Hilary. Her hand was out.

Just then, a low rumble of thunder made them look up. They hadn't realized how dark the sky had become. It hadn't started to rain yet, but it was imminent.

"We better go," said Linny, moving toward the front of the house, where they had left the bike.

"Give me the ring first!" demanded Hilary. She surprised both of them with her vehemence.

"Nope," said Linny firmly. "I found it same as you, remember?" He relented at the sight of her face. "I'll tell you what, we'll share it. I'll let you have it back tomorrow for a while."

The ring meant something to him, but he didn't know what. He couldn't explain it, even to himself. All he knew was that he wanted the ring close to him.

By the time they got home it had started to rain. At first it was a pleasant drizzle, not expected to last long. Aunt Helen had a blazing fire in the stone fireplace by the time they returned, and they had lunch on the bearskin in front of it. The three of them played the usual rainy-day Monopoly game waiting for the rain to stop.

His aunt turned from the board and said sadly to the firelight, "Remember the fun we used to have, kids? The four of us. You, Linny, and your mother against me and Hilary? My sister Josie would get so excited over these silly hotels. Like a kid. We would laugh so."

"Your turn, Aunt Helen."

The rain didn't stop. By late afternoon it was coming down in sheets. They could hear it drumming on the roof high above their heads. They couldn't see a thing out the windows; it was as if the barn were behind a waterfall.

It was still raining when they got into bed that night. Helen put an extra-fat log on the fire, the flickering light reassuring to them all. The steady drumming over their heads was unnerving. Helen had tried to call Taylor in Stratford, but the lines were down. Never had it rained so hard and so long in any of their memories.

Linny tried to joke about it, calling down from his bed in the loft, "Hey, look at me, my bed's floating."

Directly beneath him in the part of the barn that served as the dining room, Hilary lay on her narrow cot and shivered. She called up, "That's not funny, Linny. I wish I had my ring."

Her mother spoke out of the darkness of another part of the barn. "There's nothing to worry about, children. Go to sleep. You know we're on high ground here. Nothing's going to happen. It'll stop soon."

The barn was quiet except for the crackling logs.

Suddenly there was a pounding on the barn door. "Helen?" cried a voice. "Open up!"

"Taylor!" Helen quickly drew on a robe and ran to let him in. There was no mistaking the gladness in her voice.

He stepped in, his yellow slicker shedding water over the wooden floor. "Are you all right? My phone is down and I couldn't rest for worrying."

"That's so thoughtful," Helen said in almost a moan. "You came out on a night like this?" Hilary heard the surprise and gratitude, and stiffened in her bed. As if her mother weren't used to it, as if she never knew that kind of niceness. Another unfair accusation against her father!

"How did you get here?" asked her mother. "I didn't hear your car."

"I had to leave it up by the road. I couldn't take a chance getting stuck in the mud here. It's, well . . . it's something out there." He waved a hand to show how wild it was. "I'd feel a lot better if you rouse the kids and I take you to my place for the night. I expect the Battenkill will flood."

"Flood? That little piddling stream? Why, Taylor Dilt, I've been summering here all my life and I have yet to see that happen. We're fine here. You know how high above the Battenkill this barn is. My flowers down on the bottom lawn may drown, but we won't. I thank you for asking. Take off that wet thing and I'll make some coffee."

"Thank you, no, Helen. I won't stay. Walt is alone back at the house. Now that I've checked with you I can turn in myself." There was a coolness to him, a distance. Linny heard it.

"Wait, Taylor. I need to say something." Her voice dropped. What she had to say was private.

26

But Linny, in his bed, heard. Sounds rise, and what his Aunt Helen said to Taylor reached him and made him wince. They were simple words, but they echoed in Linny's head. "I'm sorry," said Aunt Helen. "Sorry about last night, what I had to tell you. It's for her sake, I hope you know that. I know I hurt you. I would hate for you to go away mad."

Go away mad. Those words cut deep.

The couple down below, talking so earnestly, faded away, and Linny saw himself repeating the scene that had haunted him for a year now.

His mother is on the couch. "Linny," she says. "Stay with me this afternoon, okay?" She pats the sofa inviting him to sit, but he doesn't. Her dark-ringed eyes look around for something to tempt him. The partly done jigsaw puzzle is spread out on the card table on the sun porch. "We'll do the puzzle together the way we used to. A race. I'll spot you ten pieces. Stay with me, Linny. All right?" There is something in her eyes, an expression Linny can't read but sees more and more often. He thinks it may be reproach. It sets him wild.

He sees himself, his own terrible face, so angry with her need of him, so angry with his own hurting heart. He hears himself yell. "The guys are waiting for me, Ma!"

The guys aren't waiting at all. He is trying to learn to skateboard and can't get the hang of it, doesn't have enough time on his own to learn. There is a skateboard tournament at the schoolyard, a contest that very after- noon. Linny desperately wants to be there, out with his friends, watching the champs, not home with her. It's all too much. He is sick and tired of her sickness.

27

"I'm going!" he yells, and he leaves and bangs the door after him.

That was the last he saw of his mother. While he was gone, that same afternoon, her heart gave way, and she was no longer on her couch when he came home. Strangers had brought her to the hospital, where she died.

He had left her alone when he should have stayed. They had parted in anger, and she would never, never know how he felt about that. She would never, never know what he had learned this past year at such cost: how much he loved her and missed her.

If only he could undo . . . Regret drenched him like sweat. Taylor was long gone, and the rain splattered on and on, until sleep delivered him from the pictures in his head.

Chapter 4

When Mrs. DeLuca turned over in her sleep the next morning, her right arm plopped down into the water. Her husband, hearing her cry out, sat up, looked around at the flooded room and then lay down again. He pulled the covers over his head. He thought he was still asleep, having a bad dream.

Mr. and Mrs. Stuart and their four kids had ice cream for breakfast. They had to wade to their freezer on the back porch, which was more than a foot underwater. The electricity was off and everything in the freezer was about to spoil. It was a shame to let good ice cream go to waste, so they ate it all. It was the happiest day of the children's lives.

The Yarn Factory, which operated right at the edge of the river, was hard hit. The rushing water carried off spools of bright colors that were intended for sweaters, but wound up twisted in the bushes for miles. Bits of red, yellow, purple, green hung like Christmas decorations along the banks. It was a gay legacy of the storm that had turned a tame brook into a tiger in a single night.

All up and down the road along the Battenkill, people awakened to flooded lawns and waterlogged houses.

It was Helen's outcry that roused Hilary and Linny that morning and brought them running to her. She was staring wide-eyed at what was out back.

The entire lower lawn was underwater. The brook that had barely come up to Linny's knees the day before had spilled over its banks. Instead of a green meadow there was a silver pond.

The river behind it was now a torrent, allowing nothing to stand in its way. Big boulders tumbled along like pebbles. The crack of rock on rock split the air like orchestra cymbals. The brook that had bubbled over those rocks now rumbled and roared, carrying along in its rush limbs of fallen trees, whole bushes, lawn chairs, children's toys. It was nature on the loose, revealing the fearful power that lies behind the glade.

The awesome sight held them all captive. It had stopped raining, but the day was gray, leaden with mist. It wasn't easy to see clearly.

"Oh, no! Look! A dog!" Hilary cried out. She thought she had seen something alive in the current. It was carried out of sight before the words were out of her mouth.

"No, I saw it. Some kid's toy," said Linny, squinting. The air was as heavy with water as a sponge. He, Hilary and Helen were wet in just the few minutes of watching. The barn itself was safe and dry, too high above the brook for flooding.

Hilary and Linny bolted breakfast so they could get out and look around.

Helen Brier went back and forth from the big double door to the back window, peering out at the weather, saying it wasn't safe, there was too much water out there, maybe the river was still cresting, telling Hilary and Linny not to go, she had this funny feeling. She continued long after they had stopped listening.

Then, when she saw there was no holding them back, she tried to delay them. First it was boots she wanted them to wear. They might have to wade. They might face deep water where they didn't expect it. There was a flood out there.

Boots in the summertime? Linny laughed. Hilary would rather die. She compromised by taking off her golf shoes and wearing sneakers, but that was only to protect her precious cleats.

Next they had to argue about wearing their rain ponchos. Then it was Hilary's tank top and shorts. "Put something on. You'll catch cold!"

"What's the matter with you, Mom?" Hilary demanded. Her mother was acting so weird over nothing. They were just going outside. The flood was over. It was a rainy day, so what? Her mother usually liked rain. What was she afraid of?

"I don't know, I don't know," Helen said, holding a hand to her forehead. She waved them away. "I'm a wreck this morning." Sudden tears reddened her eyes.

Linny averted his eyes, embarrassed. He knew it didn't have to do with their going outside. "Hey, Aunt Helen, if it means that much . . . I guess we can go later." A noise from Hilary at his side, the beginning of a squawk. He jammed an elbow at her.

His aunt swiped at the tears with the back of her hand. "Aaah, no, it's not that. Don't pay any attention to me. It was just a fight Taylor and I had the other night. You know how I hate fights. Well, not a fight exactly, more a disagreement." She glanced at Hilary. "I asked him not to come around anymore." The look she gave her daughter plainly said, There, does that satisfy you?

Color flared in Hilary's cheeks. She muttered, "C'mon, Linny, let's get going," and squatted down to check the tires on the family bike that was kept right inside the barn door.

For a long moment she stayed there, staring at nothing, biting her lips. Then the anger she was trying to suppress took over. She glared up at her mother. "Look, don't do me any favors, okay? What do I care if that creep comes over? Don't blame it on me! I'm going to live with my father, anyway!"

Without another glance at her mother she wheeled the bike out the door.

As soon as they were outside, Hilary put her hand out. "Okay, my turn," she said to Linny, still fuming. "I want my ring."

He had tried cleaning it the night before, using only soap and water and his fingers. When that didn't work he looked around the bathroom for something better. He daren't use one of Aunt Helen's towels, it would get too black. Toilet paper wouldn't do the trick. His eyes lit on his toothbrush.

As he hesitated, the ghost in his head had spoken. It urged, "Do it. You can always buy a new toothbrush. The ring might be important."

Linny had shivered. His thought exactly. He and his mother used to come up with the same thought once in a while and laugh. Now, hearing her voice only made him feel bad and in the wrong. He knew he was doomed to hear it and feel bad about it forever.

When he had finished brushing the ring with his toothbrush, the circlet was better than before, no longer black. Even though it was still badly stained, he could see that the ring was just plain brass.

He held it up to the light and on the inside rim saw some peculiar scratches. His first thought was that someone had taken a careless knife to it. But there, with a stormy night beating at the bathroom window, and in the fanciful barn that fed and quickened the imagination, it also seemed likely that the scratches might mean something, like they were some kind of funny writing.

Now, outside in broad daylight, as he faced Hilary with her hand out, his fancies of the night before seemed foolish. Not for him such superstitions. He just liked the feel of the ring. He liked to have it with him.

Reluctantly, he fished it out of his pocket and handed it to Hilary. She was ready with a shoelace. She tied it on the ring and hung it around her neck. "I get to have it tomorrow," Linny reminded her.

They had to walk the bike across the sopping field because the path was so muddy. The fog had thickened, and when they reached the road they found themselves enclosed in another world. They were inside a grayness that made ghostly shapes of the trees across the road and shut out of sight all that lay more than a few feet ahead.

They could make out the white line down the middle of the road, and they pedaled along that toward Stockville, the village that lay not more than a half mile away. The ride was disappointing, because it was too foggy to see the effects of the flood. They could hardly see anything.

On one side of the road rose a high hill they couldn't see but knew was there. The runoff from it swept across the road, seeking a lower level, searching for the sea. The water barely reached the rim of the bike wheel, yet already it was undermining the edges of the road. Bits of the black asphalt were being eaten away.

Hilary knew every bend in the road, but kept her eyes on the white line because it was so easy to stray off in the mist. She pulled up the hood of her poncho. Her hair was already soaked. She couldn't see much on either side, anyway.

"This is spooky," she murmured to Linny on the bar in front of her. There was no traffic. They passed no cars or people. "Where is everybody?" she wondered.

Linny was wondering the same thing. Wasn't anybody curious? Were they all drowned corpses bumping around in their houses? It seemed to him that he and Hilary were gliding through cotton, with everything out there blurry, hard to make out. Even the sounds that came to him seemed muffled. The thrashing of the river was a distant hum, the clash of rocks made no more noise than a cricket. The inside of his head was as quiet as the outside, everything unreal and far away at last. He loved it. He wanted the ride to last forever.

34

"What's that?" cried Hilary, and braked. She had seen some dark shapes in the middle of the road ahead. They hadn't even come yet to the Tay Café. The village was beyond that, just over the bridge.

They got off the bike and walked up to a clump of people who were standing about looking at what was happening to the road as far as they could see ahead. The water that coursed across it was a swirl of destruction. As Hilary and Linny watched, big chunks of the black ribbon were dropping off the sides of the road as if a pie were being trimmed by a knife. How far toward town this was happening no one could tell.

Sheriff Coleman was there in his yellow slicker and rain hat, a big sturdy man with a broad leathery face and a loud voice that warned everybody to go on home, get off the road, it was dangerous. "And keep your kids off it," he announced. "It's about to go any minute."

When he saw Hilary and Linny, he waved. He knew them from way back. He had once found them on the road to Jamaica, the next town over, when at the age of eight they had decided to run away, and were headed back to Brooklyn to stay with Hilly's father and see their friends.

A wind had come up, and with it gusts of rain that buffeted the other onlookers. They began to leave.

Hilary watched them go. She lifted her face to the rain and squeezed her eyes shut. Out of her private woe she cried, "I don't want to go back!"

Linny peered ahead as hard as he could. There was nothing to see through the slanted rain but a blankness, a grayness that stopped the eyes, stopped any knowing of what lay beyond.

A perverse desire seized him. It would be like going through a cloud, he thought, like skateboarding blind. It called to him.

"Hop on," he said to Hilary, and threw a leg over the bike. He was going to pedal this time. In that fog it didn't matter if he couldn't see over her head.

She expected him to turn the bike around. Instead, he stood up on the pedals and drove the bike straight ahead. She hung on, with no breath to say more than "Yay!"

Behind them Sheriff Coleman yelled plainly, "You kids! Come back here! Stop!"

That was the last clear warning Linny heard. The rest was a single horrified shout that rose from the few people still there to witness what happened.

The road directly behind him began to crumble. It fell away, following the track of the bike as if eating up the tarred roadbed for dinner. Linny plunged on into grayness, the wheels staying just ahead of the danger. He didn't notice the wind or the needles of rain on his face. He had the impression of things hurtling past him on either side, but he couldn't name them. There was a shrieking in his ears that was other than human and other than wind.

Suddenly all noise stopped. In a dense cloud he and Hilary coasted along in dead silence for a few heartbeats.

There was a lifting ahead, a lightness, a growing chatter of voices, the honking of car horns.

Then Linny and Hilary found themselves in blinding sunshine, coasting down the noisy, dirty familiar street of their old neighborhood in Brooklyn.

36

Chapter 5

➤ Linny forgot how to brake in the paralysis of the moment. He twisted the handlebars sharply to avoid collision with a someone or a something just in front of him, whether a person or a tree or a hippopotamus he couldn't say. The wheel of the bike knocked against the curb, and down he and Hilary went.

They managed to pull themselves to the curb. They sat. Linny looked over his shoulder and stared blankly at what was there but couldn't be.

It was his house, the same, the one he grew up in, the one he hadn't seen in a year because he didn't live there anymore. His mother had died in that house. In that apartment upstairs. There it was. He could see the lacy tied-back curtains, the window where his mother sat on her good days the long months that she was sick. This was his street, it was, it was, and yet it couldn't be.

Next to him Hilary made a sound in her throat. She began to rub her knees, as if an everyday act would help make sense out of where she now found herself. "What's happening?" she asked the air.

Someone pushed Linny's shoulder, somebody was saying something to him. "Hey, you guys okay? I didn't see you coming."

Linny looked up and there was Walt. Walt Dilt, somewhat shorter than he had been the day before in Vermont, a little rounder in the face, but definitely Walt. So he was in this . . . this whatever it was also.

"Oh. Hi, Walt," Linny said. It was almost funny. He nudged Hilary. "Look who's here."

Hilary cried out his name like he was a care package from home.

Walt looked down at the pair before him, obviously puzzled. He shrugged and grinned. "You know me, huh? It's great to be famous. Listen, do us a favor and move your butts. We're doing wheelies up on the curb here and you're sitting on it."

Hilary stared at him. "He doesn't know us," she said flatly.

Linny noticed Walt was wearing kneepads. He was carrying a skateboard under his arm. Nice kicktail, like the one he had at home.

At home? He *was* home! The next thought dried his mouth. Who was upstairs? Who was inside his house? He swallowed cotton.

He forced his attention back to Walt, who was talking to him as if it were perfectly natural they were here together being friendly in Brooklyn instead of being not so friendly in Vermont.

Linny tried to keep the fright that was snaking up his

middle from taking over. He said to Walt, as steadily as he could, "What is this?"

That wasn't it, so Linny began again. "What's going on here? How did you get here?"

No. That wasn't the main question. What he mainly wanted to know was: Was this real? Was he dreaming? Were they all dreaming this together?

In the next breath, without asking, he knew the answer, but he couldn't have explained it in words. He knew with cold certainty that this wasn't any dream. It was real. So what couldn't be, was. Then what did real mean?

He stood up, surprised that his legs supported him. He raised the bicycle from where it was sprawled and hung on to the handlebars.

Hilary stood also, but she was still dazed. She looked around as if she were on Mars. Then she grasped Walt's shoulder as if to make sure it was solid. She shook it, wanting something from him. She wanted him to set things straight. "Come on, Walt. Quit it. How did we all get here?"

Walt shifted his skateboard and gave a short burst of laughter. He said, " 'We'? What are you, kidding me? I live here!"

He saw the bewilderment on their faces and tried to clear up some misunderstanding. "I mean, not here exactly," he said. "Over that way." He waved vaguely. I don't know this block. My dad is working around here, so I came over. Hey, we're practicing for the tournament. Do you mind?" He was nudging them away from where they had landed. He was finished with them.

Two other boys in the middle of the street were concentrating on skateboard maneuvers, practicing tricks, watching one another put on a show.

One of them looked over at the trio and called out, "Hey, Linny, you're gonna get it. Your mom was yelling for you."

The other said, "Hey, you and Hilly gonna take a shower together in them things? Whoooey!"

Linny looked down at himself and at his cousin. They still had on their ponchos and there was no sign of rain. The sun was high. He nodded dumbly, recognizing Eddie Gilberto and dopey Silverman. The guys on the street. They used to hang out together. In the same class. He hadn't seen them for a year and they were talking to him as if they'd seen him yesterday. They looked exactly the same, but exactly, same clothes and everything.

Walt shook Hilary's arm as if she were sleepwalking and he had to wake her up. "Are you all right?"

She looked at him and laughed aloud at such a question.

From an upstairs window of the house behind them, a voice cried, "Linny! I've been waiting. What took you so long!"

Hilary, not Linny, was able to look up. In a faint voice she said, "Hi, Aunt Josie." She took hold of Linny's trembling hand. "It's your mother up there."

Full of surprise and gladness her aunt cried out her name. "Hilly! I can't believe it. Come! Come!" The head withdrew and the window closed.

Linny and Hilary stared at one another wildly and then clung for a long moment.

"In a minute," whispered Linny. "I can't yet."

Whatever had befallen them, for whatever reason, they were here, and that was his mother upstairs. He was going to see her again.

They dropped their ponchos and huddled together in the hallway on one of the steps that led upstairs. Neither of them could mount the stairs.

Linny's mother called down to them from the landing: "What are you doing here, Hilary? Come tell me everything. No wonder Linny's been gone so long. Come up. I'm dying for my tea."

Linny climbed the stairs, pulling himself up step by step like an old person. He stood before his mother pierced beyond tears, unable to talk, taking in air, swallowing, trying to manage the moment. He wanted only to look at her. That was her face, moving, speaking. That was her voice, the voice he had heard in his head all year, his ghost. Only now not a ghost. The scarfs she wore around her throat and over her shoulders lifted with her breath. He drew in her scent.

She was saying something to him. Her hand was out. He finally heard the word "tea." She was wanting something from him. Then her hand dropped. "You forgot!" she said, in the dramatic, overcharged way that used to set his teeth on edge. There were actual tears in her eyes.

"Sorry," stumbled out of his mouth. He could have said it a million times and it wouldn't have been enough. She must have sent him to the store for her special herb tea and he hadn't returned with it. "Sorry, Mom," he said, wanting her name in his mouth.

Hilary shot him a wild glance and guided her aunt inside and to the sofa in the living room, which was her daytime bed.

Linny trailed after them. The girl straightened the sheets and picked up the crocheted afghan from the rug and tucked it around her aunt. Like Linny, she wasn't hearing a word her aunt was saying; her mind was racing, going noplace, like a rat in a maze.

Finally she placed her hand across her aunt's mouth and said to her, "Aunt Josie, tell me something. Are we in heaven?"

Josie Erda turned dark-ringed eyes to Hilary, and for the moment that it took for amusement to gather, the sick, querulous lines around her mouth and forehead disappeared. Good humor and approval were there instead, and Linny yearned toward her. He wanted that look for himself. He stared at his mother the way starving people stare at food.

"Honestly, Hilly," Josie said, "you are better for me than medicine. What a way to put it. Well, I'm glad to see you too." She patted the sofa. "Sit. Tell me, how is it my sister didn't let me know you were coming? Wait a minute." She gazed up at her son. "Please, Linny, the tea. The health food store. Remember?"

She began to cough, and now patted the sofa as if searching for something. With one hand covering her mouth, she waved the other at Linny, who went immediately to the spindly desk by the far wall, where he remembered she kept some of her things handy. He rummaged and pulled out a fresh handkerchief. He remembered ironing it.

His mother pressed it to her lips and took a few slow breaths before continuing. She shook the handkerchief at Hilly. "He always knows what I want, my son. Were you ever here when we played that game? He was just a little kid. What did we call it, Linny? You know what I mean."

Linny's inward eye flashed an image of his younger self at the kitchen table and his mother, healthy and laughing, standing over him. He was supposed to guess what she had in mind for his breakfast. No matter what crazy thing he said, she would be astounded that he had guessed it. One of their games.

" 'Mind reader.' We used to call it 'mind reader,' Mom."

"That's it!" Then a shadow passed over her face. Her pleased look went away and the sick look returned. She said to him, "A mind reader who forgets a small favor for his mother."

The spurt of guilt in Linny was automatic and entirely familiar.

"Go, Linny," she said. "Remember, chamomile tea, the store brand, no other. Also, while you're at it, bring us some of their oat bran cookies. None of your junk food for us, right, Hilary? We'll celebrate. You have enough money?"

He shook his head. No money. He must have lost it. Then in a dizzy rush he realized how nutty that thought was. He had to hang on to what he knew, or thought he knew.

It was still summer. But what summer? His mother was still alive—but he saw and now understood what the dark circles under her eyes meant, and what the pasty skin and the effort to draw breath meant.

But what was the date now? If this was August, as it had been when he woke up that morning in Vermont, then it was the month she had died. How many days left?

With that thought, he grew afraid of his feelings. He threw Hilary a desperate glance and said to her, not his mother, "I'll be right back."

He was glad for the errand. He had to get out, where he could draw a breath, maybe think this through. Or maybe scream down the heavens. He had to get hold of himself, get away from the terrible joy of his live mother. He couldn't think beyond that. If he stayed a minute longer he would be on his knees with his head in her lap.

Chapter 6

Linny leaped down the stairs two at a time. Once outside he stood at the curb staring down at his filthy sneakers, dried mud from the Vermont storm that morning still coating the sides. He took deep breaths and exhaled through his mouth like a long-distance runner.

His mother was upstairs. Slowly, through his veins, a warmth began to spread, easing a chill in his bones he hadn't known he had. He was back! Never mind how. There must be an explanation, some part of his mind insisted, but right now he didn't care. He was here. His mother was alive and the past year was dead.

This incredible fact went straight to his heart and sent a pulse of joy shooting through his blood. His head lifted and he filled his lungs with the tarry summer smell of his old street.

The story of the wooden boy Pinocchio jumped into his mind. *Pinocchio* used to be a favorite book of his when he was little. He could see the very page that showed the puppet all broken up, legs and arms every which way. Then he was rebuilt, put together again. That's how Linny felt. Put together again.

But this time he would do different, be different. His mind flooded with all the things he would do now. He wouldn't be impatient, ever. No matter what she said now. He would stay with her and take care and not talk back, not fight.

This time she wouldn't die. Maybe if he had stayed with her that last day her heart wouldn't have given up. This time he wouldn't leave her.

He had another chance!

The rolling wheels of the skateboards and the shouts of the boys in the street cut through his thoughts.

"Hey, what's so funny?" yelled Eddie Gilberto as he sailed past Linny, standing sidewise on the deck of his skateboard.

Linny shook his head quickly. He hadn't realized he was smiling.

Across the street Danny Silverman had lined up some orange cones in front of the parked cars and was weaving in and out of them. He rode goofy foot, Linny noticed, right foot up front. And with no helmet or pads. Figures, he said to himself dryly. Danny Silverman begged for accidents the way dogs beg for bones. This was one of the few times Linny remembered seeing him without a bandage someplace.

He looked around for Walt Dilt. He called to Eddie, "Where's that kid who was here? Walt?"

Eddie Gilberto shrugged and said to Linny, "Hey, look at this. Eat your heart out!" In the middle of the street he did a kick-turn, and then rode by Linny with his skinny arms outspread. He ended with a fanfare for himself. "Ta-daa!"

Danny Silverman suddenly stepped off his board and ran with it to the sidewalk. "Cops!" he yelled to Eddie from the curb.

Before Eddie could react, a police car cruised up. A curly-haired policeman stuck his rosy face out the window and beckoned to Eddie. "Come over here, kid." The boy tucked his board under his arm and went to the passenger side.

"Don't you know it's illegal to ride them things in the street? Also dangerous. Huh? You know that?"

"Gimme a break, we don't have traffic here! We was just practicing for the meet, right, Silverman? There's gonna be a competition at the school. Me and my friend, we look out for cars all the time."

His friend Danny had just developed a keen interest in the sparrows sitting aloft on the telephone lines.

The policeman grinned at Eddie. "Well, do your practicing on the sidewalk. Else in the schoolyard around the corner, whatever. No street 'boarding, you hear? Practicing for a meet, huh? You'll be meat if you don't keep those things out of the street. A car could run right up your tailpipe. Don't let me catch you again."

A look of immense relief spread over Eddie's face as the police car prepared to cruise on. He bobbed his head and said, "Okay, okay, I hear you."

The driver braked, leaned over and said something to his partner. He pointed to the orange cones set up in a line alongside the parked cars.

The policeman whistled at Danny to catch his attention. The boy still had his head in the air, pretending not to notice what was going on. He was just an innocent bystander.

"Hey, you! You know something about those traffic cones?"

Danny looked around to see whom the cop was talking to. "Who, me?" he asked, pointing to himself with an air of astonishment.

"Yeah, you. Come over here, son. Tell me all about them."

"What cones?" asked Danny, looking right, left, at the sky, at the rooftops. Anyplace but two feet in front of him, where the orange cones were lined up.

The rosy-faced cop laughed and said, "Never mind, we'll see that they're collected. They're city property, not toys."

When the police drove off, Eddie was enraged. He yelled at his friend, "Hey, Silverman, thanks a lot! You were a lotta help. Next time I'm gonna hand you to the cops on a platter. You weren't even wearing your safety, and I'm the one that gets it. And now we're gonna lose the cones. Get them outta there before the cops come back again."

Linny was thinking about the skateboard tournament Eddie had mentioned. Walt Dilt had said something about it also. Could it be the same one he had gone to the year before?

"Hey, that skateboard tournament? When is it going to be?" he asked.

Eddie sneered. "What's it to you, Erda? It's only for

people who can ride, so you know where that leaves you. Sitting on your butt with the rest of the losers. And last week you said you wouldn't come watch if they paid you. Make up your mind, why don'tcha?"

"Well, when is it again?"

Eddie gave him a disgusted look. "Saturday. Over at the school. You forgot already? Hey, Silverman, Linny's getting to be as dopey as you."

He and Eddie Gilberto used to be the same height, but now Linny was conscious of looking down a bit. He could see the top of his friend's dirty-blond hair where it stood up like a brush. Yet Eddie didn't seem to notice the difference. It occurred to Linny that his mother also hadn't said anything to him about the fact that his clothes were different or that he had grown. He must look the same to her.

All of a sudden, his old buddy seemed childish. He had never thought so before. Eddie was two months older than he was. Or at least he used to be. But now Linny was the one who was older, or was he? If he and Hilary had returned to a time in the past, he must be.

But what time had they returned to? He had to find out what year this was for sure. This morning, when he woke up to the flood, it was Wednesday, August 7, 1991. He was sure of that because the night before he had boarded the bus to Vermont, his father had sat on the edge of the bed they had to share in that awful rooming house and reminded him of a looming date.

"Just a few more days, son. Next Sunday, August 11, and don't you forget it. I'll be in North Carolina and you'll be with your Aunt Helen, but we'll both think of your mother, won't we? One single year she's been gone." His father had run his palm over his face and Linny could see behind the glasses that the pale eyes were bloodshot. He was in a panic for fear that he was about to see his father cry.

Linny remembered that day only too well. He had come home to an empty house and neighbors standing around outside. The ambulance had taken his mother away and he never saw her again.

But right now she was upstairs, alive still. If it was last year, it couldn't yet be the eleventh. His head swam with possibilities of this.

What was the date today!

Linny looked up to the cloudless sky as if the shining sun would tell him. It was summertime, that he knew. Out of all the days of his past, what day was this?

Eddie was examining his skateboard closely. It was made of wood and had a bad ding on one of the edges. "Gotta sand this," he said, smoothing the gouge tenderly.

"Yeah," agreed Linny. "Hey, what's today, Eddie? You know the date? I forget." He couldn't ask what year this was. They would put him in the funny farm for sure.

"Sure, I know the date. Fourteen ninety-two. You know what? Tomorrow Columbus is going to discover America."

Linny thought to himself with true astonishment, Did I ever really think this jerk was funny? Aloud, he said patiently, "Okay, forget it, Gilberto. So where do you sign up for the tournament?"

Eddie shook his head and sailed off, circling his ear

with a finger a few times, meaning to tell the world that Lionel Erda had lost his marbles.

Linny called to Danny Silverman who was busy piling up the orange cones on the sidewalk before hiding them someplace. "Hey, Danny, where do you sign up for the skateboard meet?" Linny knew it was safe to ask Silverman.

The thickset boy straightened, snuffed up another load and said earnestly, "Over at the school. They let beginners? I didn't know that."

Linny was in the grip of an idea, a wish, almost a summons. Last time he went he was a watcher; this time he'd be a contestant. Last time his mother stayed home and died; this time she'd be with him and live. He would win the tournament! This last year of concentrated practice would pay off. He'd show Gilberto. Most of all, he'd keep his mother with him and show her what he could do.

"You have a board to lend me, Silverman? An extra?"

"Yeah, my old one, you know, the Hassan Tracker. It's got a crack."

Linny didn't listen past the "yeah." He was already planning ahead. He would sign up. He would bring all he had learned this whole past year, when his board was his best outside friend. All those months of scraped knees and elbows would be worth it. He had pushed himself harder and faster down the twisty hills of Frick Park for just this moment. He would win, and his mother would be there to see it.

He heard the yelling of the crowd in his ears, just for him, because he had won the tournament. He saw himself wave only at her even though everybody was clapping and trying to get his attention. She smiled back at him, and good humor and health and approval shone from her face, and nobody was mad at anybody.

The image burst as the thought of his mother reminded him that she was waiting upstairs for her tea! He flew down the street to Tremont and headed for Sunnyside health food store at the end of the block. On the way he stopped at Concetta's newspaper store, where the papers were stacked outside. His eye fell eagerly on the date. Wednesday, August 8, 1990.

He was back a year! The eleventh was Saturday. The same day as the tournament. The day she had died. He had three more days!

Chapter 7

Hilary ran out of Linny's house in what could only be described as a state of bliss.

A few minutes before, her cousin had burst in with the bag of cookies and tea in one hand and a newspaper in the other. Hilary had followed Linny's trembling finger as he showed her the date on the paper.

So now she knew. Aunt Josie had wanted her to stay for lunch, but she had to go home. "Your father won't be home in the middle of the day!" her aunt called after her as she ran down the stairs. Yeah, but maybe he will.

It was like floating, Hilary decided. Happiness made you float. She was headed home. Her feet went where she wanted them to go without tripping her. She didn't bump into one single person on the way, because she was floating, carried along by the joy of this unexpected gift. By some miracle, by some magic, she was back a whole year. And because she was back a year her father was still home. A year before, he hadn't left them yet.

No, no, she corrected herself. Her father hadn't left them. He would never do that. It was her mother. She had driven him away. But that was then and this was now.

Hilary giggled aloud at that as she loped along, causing a few passersby to glance curiously at the big, happy girl. She had it backward. In the present circumstances, she would have to say that was now and this was then. It was crazy, it was impossible, but however you said it, here she was, and soon she would see her father again. He wasn't in California, he was home.

She jogged and skipped, breathing in the sun-warmed air as if it were wine. The cracked sidewalk she bounded on seemed particularly beautiful, with all those glints of embedded mica. She had never noticed them before. How good to feel the sun on her head, what a nice day, how pretty the window boxes along the street, those cheery little gardens that lifted the faces of the brick houses. The only thing missing were her golf cleats. She imagined wearing them, hearing their clickety-clack as she walked, a rhythmic beat that matched the tripping of her heart.

As she turned the corner of her own street she stopped. She needed a moment to catch up with herself. She needed to sort out in her mind what was happening. What had happened.

She sat down on the steps of the nearest house. It was one of a long row of attached brick houses stretching down the block, each like the others, with four white stone steps to the front door and a tree at the curb tamed by a wire mesh. Her house was halfway down the block, but she wasn't quite ready to go there yet.

She propped her chin on her hand but couldn't think. She couldn't get her head to work. "You have just entered the Twilight Zone," she said in a whisper, and almost burst out laughing again. She usually was spooked listening to that program on TV. She enjoyed goose bumps. And now that she was truly in the twilight zone, or whatever zone you could call it, she felt more gleeful than scared.

Here she was, living a miracle, her own fairy tale, a whopper. She had always adored fairy tales and secretly believed in them, or rather, wanted to believe in them, despite all contrary evidence. She wanted to believe that people lived "happily ever after," and that a special providence was looking after her. Okay, maybe not a fairy godmother, but she had always had this deep-down feeling that she was marked and special and that nothing bad could happen to her.

Yet she had lost that feeling of being Providence's child these past long months. She had lost her father to divorce. Bad things could happen, even to her. There was no special protection for her.

And now, here she was, sitting on the steps of a house on her street in Brooklyn, when just that morning she had awakened in the barn in Vermont. Magic! Her Aunt Josie was alive! Magic. A year had dropped away, and she and Linny were back to before the bad things happened. They had fallen through some rabbit hole, some hole in Time. Her cousin might find some logical explanation for it, but to her it was all magic. She was a child again, dazed and believing.

Her head perked up and she looked around at where

she was, her sight sharpened by the novelty of seeing her own block in the summertime. All her life she had spent her summers at the barn.

It was so much quieter than usual. Not so many cars, not so much bustle, as if the whole neighborhood were in neutral, idling in the sun. There were some little kids down farther, playing hopscotch on the sidewalk, their cries barely reaching her.

None of her friends was to be seen, and she was glad for that. She didn't want to explain anything. First she had to explain it to herself. She turned her mind to what could have made them take this leap backward in time.

What was the beginning? She saw herself and Linny in the abandoned house. They had found the ring. Oh yes, that was the start. The ring. Then the flood. Then the fight with her mother over Taylor, Hilary hating them both. She and Linny on the bike riding the ghostly road to Stockville. Then what?

Yells. Sheriff Coleman and the other people were yelling at them to go back. No, no, she didn't want to. This tremendous push to go on, to leave behind her scrambled feelings toward home—she had felt it with all her heart. Then, as if her wish had become sound and Linny had heard it, he rode on into the fog and wind and rain.

She saw herself and Linny on the bike. In her mind's eye her hand rose to clasp the ring under her poncho. She felt the smooth roundness of it as if it were in her hand that very moment.

Oh yes, the ring was the start. It was why they were here. It was their magic.

56

Her hand went to the string around her neck that held it. The shoelace was there, but the ring was gone!

She stood up and shook out her tank top, thinking that perhaps it had fallen down inside her shirt. She jumped up and down hoping to shake it out of her shorts.

Maybe it had been torn from her in the storm as she and Linny cycled down the crumbling road.

Hilary put her whole mind back once again to riding those handlebars through the wind and rain. She had had hold of the ring when they started out, and it was with her as they had plunged on.

Then what? They had come out of the storm to Linny's old street and toppled over Walt Dilt. Maybe she had lost it then. If so, it would still be there. She had to retrace her steps.

Hilary ran back to Linny's house. The skateboarding boys were still wheeling around in the middle of the street. She began to search inch by inch the black asphalt where she and Linny had fallen from the bike. The spot was near the granite curb, but not quite, because she recalled having to walk a few steps before sitting down. Maybe the ring was under the litter backed up against the curb. She turned over candy wrappers, soda cans, matchbook covers. She searched farther away, bent over, eyes on the ground, looking closely and vainly for the lost ring.

Eddie Gilberto halted his board to say, "Whatcha looking for?"

"I must have dropped this ring I was wearing around here someplace."

"What is it? An engagement ring? Someone give you

diamonds?" Eddie checked her out to see if she knew how funny he was.

"Yeah, diamonds, Eddie." Hilary let him know she knew a dumb remark when she heard one.

"So good luck. It's probably down the sewer by now." Eddie pushed on his board, flat-tracking down the street.

"Hey, Danny," Hilary called to the other boy, who was sitting on the curb across the street watching her without curiosity. "Have you seen sort of a big ring around here someplace? I mean a real big one, like too big for a finger but you couldn't get your hand through?" It was hard to describe.

Danny took in the question and then shook his head. No, he hadn't seen any ring.

Well, that was that. Hilary had searched as best she could. Maybe Eddie was right, maybe it had rolled down the sewer. Maybe it had just disappeared. All she knew was that she and Linny didn't have it anymore, and that made her feel shaky. She sensed rather than reasoned that the ring was terribly important to them. It had gotten them there. Without it . . . who knows? She had better tell Linny.

Danny raised his head again. He said to her, "Maybe it wasn't money he found. I thought maybe it was."

"What are you talking about?" Hilary noticed a kind of flatness about Danny's eyes that she had never noticed when she used to play around here with Linny. Since her aunt had died and her cousin had moved away there was no reason for her to come to this block. Now that she thought about it, there was more sharpness to Eddie's face than Danny's. She hadn't realized you could see smartness looking out of the eyes. It gave her a kick to realize that being a year older made her see that.

Danny said, "That other guy, the one that was here before. He found something, I saw him. He picked something up and put it in his pocket. I asked him how much money. He wouldn't show me. I don't know. Maybe it was a ring." He shrugged. Who cared about rings.

He must mean Walt Dilt! Hilary thought. "Oh, Danny, thanks! Do you know where Walt lives?"

"Who?"

"The other guy, Walt Dilt. The one you're talking about, who found something here in the street. I want to ask him if it was my ring. You know where he lives?"

Danny had no idea.

Never mind. She and Linny would find him easy.

Hilary stood under Linny's window and called up to him as she had done so many times before. His face appeared at the window and she motioned to him to come on down.

As he stepped out his front door Linny said to her, "What are you doing here? I thought you couldn't wait to get home." He saw how distressed she was. "What's the matter?"

"I lost the ring! It's gone!" She showed him the empty shoelace.

In an attempt to hide his own dismay over the unexpected news he said, "Is that all! Whew. I thought it was something important."

Hilary looked at him and said nothing.

Linny hadn't considered the role of the ring in this wild experience of theirs. She was probably making a big deal over nothing. Nevertheless, he couldn't deny an upsurge of alarm.

"Did you look around?"

"Yes, I did! But you look too."

They both prowled around for a while, repeating what Hilary had done. They sifted through the assorted trash blown against the curb and ranged the area where the bike had toppled.

When it was clear that the ring was not to be found, Hilary told Linny what Danny Silverman had told her. "So I'm hoping maybe Walt Dilt has it. We have to find him, Linny. Where did he say he lived?"

"He didn't say. He just sort of waved, remember? Over that way. Now how would we find out? I'll go ask Eddie."

It didn't take long for Linny to return, shaking his head, letting Hilary know he hadn't found out a thing.

"Eddie says he just shows up once in a while. Never even bothered to ask his name. The only clue is that Walt told him this block was better than his own for riding. So now all we have to do is find a bumpy street. You think Brooklyn has any bumpy streets?"

At that moment, Hilary was assailed by so many contrary emotions that she felt suddenly exhausted. The events of the day were catching up to her. She had been transported back to when her father was her father and it was wonderful, but in a world where such things could happen, anything at all could happen. The ring was something she needed to have hold of, like an anchor in a whirlwind, like something or someone watching over them. And yet she had lost it. What did that mean for them?

She couldn't take it all in. If only she didn't feel so fuzzy in the head, as if she needed a nap. But the last thing she wanted was to sleep. If she did, maybe she would wake up and be back in Vermont!

No, she didn't want that to happen . . . yet.

Linny, who was standing moodily by her side, digging the toe of his sneaker in the sidewalk, made a sharp sound of surprise in his throat. He said, "I forgot! Didn't Walt say his father had a workshop around here someplace? We know Taylor was a carpenter. That's a big clue! All we have to do is find out where there's a carpenter's workshop in this neighborhood, right? So we'll ask around. Somebody will know. It shouldn't be so hard."

Hilary looked at him admiringly. What a brain. She felt much better, full of optimism again. They would find Walt Dilt and he would give them back the ring.

"When?" she wanted to know.

Linny had already turned away to go back upstairs. "When what?" He knew very well what she was asking.

"When are we going to look for Walt?"

Linny looked up to his mother's window. "Hilly, I can't just now. I don't want to. I can't even believe she'll be there when I go back upstairs right now. I can't believe anything. Know what I mean? It's all . . ." He circled a finger around his temple.

Hilary, who believed everything, nodded. She knew what it was to have your head spin like a merry-go-round. "So, what are you saying? We're not going to look for the ring, or what?"

"No, I mean not this minute. Later, okay? Or how about tomorrow? If we are still here tomorrow, we'll go around the neighborhood." He didn't want to tell her that he wasn't about to leave his mother alone for anything, not even the ring. All he wanted was to go back upstairs now and fix his eyes on her, touch her dress, hear her voice.

That was okay with Hilary. Now that they had a clue to follow, she could wait. In the meantime maybe her father was home.

Chapter 8

Hilary retraced her steps homeward; only this time, instead of the giddy sense of anticipation she had had earlier, a vague unease had set in, the way a small cloud can coat the sun. She told herself it was because of the lost ring.

She fixed her mind on what was waiting for her the minute her father saw her.

A tiny doubt walked into her mind, an unwelcome guest. Maybe he wouldn't come home tonight. It was possible. Hilly tried to think when it was that her mother had been paranoid about some lady in his office. She had been proven wrong, of course. Hilly had overheard her father swearing on a stack of Bibles that it wasn't so. But there could be a million other reasons for him to be out tonight. Please, no. Let him come home after work and find her there.

Hilly could see the surprise pop open his sandy eyes, and then that great smile would spread over his face, the famous smile that said this was the best thing that could ever happen to him, whatever it was. No one could resist it. His arms would open when he saw her, and she would be drawn close and once again smell his special smell of clean shirt and sweat and the smoky, medicine smell of drink. A father smell. Hers.

She quickened her steps. She couldn't wait.

Her old familiar street was so quiet in the afternoon heat that it gave her the feeling it was as expectant as she, holding its breath in sympathy. The leaves on the spindly trees along the curb hardly moved. She wondered if everyone was inside taking a nap. The little kids who had been playing outside a short time before were gone now. Everything was so hushed. Maybe they were all inside eating lunch, but it was way past lunchtime. It must be mid-afternoon by now.

That reminded her. She was starved. She hadn't had a thing to eat since breakfast at the barn this morning.

Just this morning? She marveled. It seemed like a year ago. No, a year from now, she corrected herself, no longer truly knowing what was when. Time travel was hungry work.

As she bounded up her own front steps she noticed the red geraniums that her mother loved and planted each year were in full bloom in the window boxes. Hilary said to herself that she would tell her mother how pretty they looked.

Then she remembered.

Her mother had always planted them right before they left for the barn in June. She claimed that they were brave, hardy flowers and protected her home while she was in

Vermont. Every Labor Day, the red flowers at the windows were the first things her mother looked for when they arrived home from the country.

This year she hadn't planted any. When they had left for the barn this past June the boxes were empty. Her mother had said she had no heart for them anymore. They hadn't protected her home at all. Her sister was dead and her husband gone.

But look, here they were, bright as flags! The bad things hadn't happened yet. Aunt Josie was still alive and Hilary's father lived in this house and there was nothing to cry over; everything was fixed and the world was right again. Except that Hilary had lost the ring. But maybe her father could fix that too.

She turned the doorknob and put her shoulder to the door. It was locked. That meant her father wasn't home from the agency yet. Probably he was showing a client around. The real estate office where he worked kept him odd hours. He could be home any minute or not till late. That was one of the troubles. He never said, never phoned. Her mother blamed it on other women. She couldn't see that he was a free spirit, as he always said he was.

Hilly went to the courtyard out back and managed to reach her bedroom window by standing on a crate from the garage. As she expected, the window was open and she was able to crawl in. Her father was never careful about locking up.

The house smelled musty and unaired. She looked around her bedroom curiously, not knowing for that split second what was wrong. Something was.

Then she noticed the Guns N' Roses poster still up there on the wall. Of course. This was her old room, her room of the year before. She knew because she had torn that poster down on the rotten rainy day when she had that fight with her mother. It was when the first postcard had come, sometime last October. Her father was sending love to his princess from California. Her mother had an industrial-strength fit when Hilary said she was going to hitch out there to stay with him, and that's what the fight was about.

And on the white chenille bedspread, resting on the pillow, was her old Cabbage Patch doll. She hadn't seen it for ages. Her mother must have given it away after the big discovery. Hilary picked the doll up and sure enough, there it still was, the quarter-size cigarette burn on the spread that the doll was meant to hide.

Hilary sat on the edge of the bed with the doll in her hands and had to smile at the remembrance. How frantic they were, she and her best friend, Nancy, as the glowing end dropped off the shared cigarette onto the bedspread. How they walloped that bed, slapping and beating, trying to keep the hole from spreading. There wasn't a blaze, she recalled, but there sure was a stink. She could still smell it.

What a dope she was then. How much older and wiser she was now. She and Nancy were ten-year-olds, what could you expect? At eleven you know so much more. What did she think, that her mother wouldn't notice the hole if the doll sat there? Hilary had to laugh at herself. Her mother had been okay about the whole thing, she had to admit. Didn't make a big deal out of it, just showed her some disgusting pictures of an old smoker's lungs. As if that could ever happen to her.

Hilary put back the doll covering the hole and left the room. She had enough of her old self. She wondered if you always looked back at what you were and thought to yourself, How dumb.

The first real thrill came when she saw that the kitchen was a mess. Her father certainly had been home the night before. Pots and dishes were soaking in the sink, not even in the dishwasher yet. There were open canisters, uncapped bottles, spice jars, signs of her father's cooking all over the place. He loved to cook, but cleaning up after himself was another matter.

Peering into the sink she noticed that her father must have had company the night before. There were too many dishes for just one person, and still on the counter were two wineglasses. Maybe he saved the dirty dishes for a few nights and put them in the dishwasher all at once. She would clean up after she had something to eat.

Hilary made herself a couple of peanut butter sandwiches and wandered around the house, going from room to room. She was home again, back to when things were still good. She was seeing it all with older eyes, knowing all that had happened in the intervening year. Bad things.

When she came to her parents' bedroom and saw the rumpled sheets and the indentation of her father's head on the pillow, she couldn't bear it any longer. She threw herself on the bed, burrowed her head in the pillow she knew was his, and gave way to tears, the pent-up emotion of the whole miraculous day.

Eventually the long sobs became short ones, the tears

began to slow, and soon what was left of the storm was an occasional catch of indrawn breath.

Hilary fell asleep, worn out by it all.

She was awakened by a crash. She lifted her head from the pillow with a start. It sounded as if something had dropped and broken—like glass. It came from someplace in the apartment, most likely the kitchen. Unless someone was ripping them off, her father had come home!

The blinds were up. She could see that it was still light out, so she couldn't have slept long. Yet the clock beside the bed said six twenty-three. She had been asleep for hours!

Now she heard a loud voice roaring a string of curses at whatever had happened. It was her father! He always had an imaginative way with curses. It was one of the few things he did that her mother actually enjoyed. She used to say he was a curse artist and should sell them for money, he would make a fortune.

Hilary could tell from his tone that he wasn't really angry. It was for show-off. He had an audience.

Hearing his voice after so long made her eyes sting again, only this time with sheer joy. She raised herself from the bed and quietly stole out of the room. She would surprise him.

Her own feet betrayed her. What she didn't remember was to lift them. She stumbled over the rug in the hall and fell with a crash across the entry of the kitchen.

Her father was holding a drink in his hand. At Hilary's appearance the glass leaped out of his hand, did a little spin in the air and joined another glass in pieces on the floor.

A female screamed, but it wasn't Hilary. The scream came from a well-dressed woman in a white summer suit who had been sitting at the small breakfast table moments before, but had been pulled to her feet by Hilary's entrance. She stared at the fallen girl with bulging eyes in which fright was giving way to amusement.

"Holy Mary, mother of God," breathed Hilary's father, shocked into reverence.

Hilary scrambled to her feet and fell on her father like a big clumsy puppy, almost knocking him over. She threw her arms around his neck. "Daddy," she cried. "Daddy, Daddy."

"Hey, let me breathe, hang on there," he said, forcing a little laugh, like a man utterly taken aback and trying to hide it. He pulled his daughter's arms away and held her at arm's length to look at her.

His hair was as crinkled as Hilary's, only the dark was spattered with gray. He wore it combed straight back and long enough to curl around his collar. He was a big-shouldered man in shirtsleeves and loosened tie, with the easy, smooth moves of a man light on his feet and confident of his charm. There was a belly growing under his shirt, but he was still handsome in a heavy-featured way. His coarse, good-humored face—wide nose, black brows, heavy cheeks—softened as he gazed at his daughter.

"Of all the surprises in the world," he began. "Does your mother know you're here?" He quickly looked past Hilary to the doorway as if he expected an apparition to appear. "She here? She with you?"

"No, no, Daddy, she's at the barn. I'm here with Linny. Wait till I tell you!"

He didn't give her a chance. Relief had him grab her to him and then turn her to his companion. "Delly, I want you to meet my princess, the sweetest kid in the world. Hilary, this is Mrs. Malkin. She's a newcomer to the office—right, Delly? I'm showing her the ropes."

Mrs. Malkin had sat herself down again and was watching the reunion with a tight smile. She crossed her legs and broadened her smile into a full show of pink gums. "Hi there. Pleased, I'm sure. That was some entrance. You took ten years off my life. Talk about scared. Next time, have a heart, give a person some warning or something."

Hilary had to giggle a little but kept her eyes averted from the woman. She was too embarrassed to look at her because she already loathed everything about her. She didn't like her gummy smile, or the green eye makeup, or her jokes. But mainly it was just her being there, the way she was sitting. This person was too much at home.

Hilary was bursting to tell her father the strange events that had brought her here. "Daddy, wait till you hear! You can't imagine!"

"I'm listening, sweetheart. Delly, I ask you, is this a beauty I have here, or what? And smart? C'mon, princess, let's do our waltz for Mrs. Malkin. She thinks she's seen dancing. Wait till she gets a load of this."

Sneakers off, Hilary's bare feet on top of his, his strong arm around her waist, off they went, waltzing around the kitchen and then into the dark living room. Hilly was in heaven. This is how it used to be. For as long as she could remember, they had danced together like that, his feet under hers, him leading her around and around as if they were ballroom partners. Sometimes they danced to records, sometimes to his pleasant baritone that knew the words to every big-band song that ever was. She remembered looking up at him from somewhere around his knees. Now they were eye to eye, but the pride and flutter that had filled her then filled her now.

Mrs. Malkin followed them into the living room and switched on the lights. She slouched against the wall watching them, an indulgent smile on her big bored face.

She looked at her watch. "I hate to break this up, Hal, but there's that, uh, meeting you wanted to get to. Unless, of course, you changed your mind. Up to you."

"No, no, be right with you, Delly." He dropped his arms, releasing Hilary in order to check his watch. "Whew. You're right. We're running late."

"Gotta go, sweetheart," he said to Hilary. At the sight of her face he added, "Now look, baby, you can't just appear and expect me to drop everything. There's a very important business meeting on tonight. Something I have to get to."

There was a small, silent exchange between Hilary's father and his lady friend. Mrs. Malkin shook her blond head slightly and shrugged. Her father's eyes insisted yes.

Hilary was quick to see this. She cried, "No, Daddy, you don't understand! You don't know what's happened. You left! I haven't seen you!" she wailed.

Her father's hearty laugh covered her protests. He said to the woman, over Hilary's head, "What can you do when you're a star in your own family? I was up to Vermont two weeks ago, would you believe it? And she says she hasn't seen me."

71

With a gesture he indicated that Hilary was to pick up the pieces of glass on the floor. As she was sweeping them up he said to her bent head, "You know I hate it up there. Always have. Give me the beach anytime, what do you say, Delly? Sun, sand, look at the ocean, beautiful. I can relax on the beach. That barn . . . well, my wife likes it. Nothing to do there, absolutely zip, except count the bugs. But I go. Don't I go, Hilly? I go because my little girl, my princess, is up there. So don't give me that not-seeing-me jazz."

The corners of his mouth went up, but he wasn't really smiling. He shook an admonitory finger. "You don't want to start laying that guilt stuff on me, baby. I've had it up to here with that." The last part was said meaningfully to the other woman.

Hilary emptied the dustpan of broken glass into the trash. She looked at her father woefully. "I'm not, I'm not!" That wasn't it at all. How to explain and keep him? How to get his attention? She stamped her foot passionately. "I'm just . . . It's only . . ."

Her father looked again at his watch and reached for his jacket, which was draped over a chair. Briskly he said, "I tell you what. I'll drop you off at Josie's. Stay the night. Yeah, better stay the night. I don't know how late the meeting will go on, and I don't want you here alone. Come on, Delly, we have to get going."

He was moving them out of the kitchen, shepherding them with widespread arms, shutting off lights as they went. He said to Hilary, "I'll call you in the morning, sweetheart. We'll make a date. Definitely. I'm going to plan something that will knock your socks off.

"Listen, do me a favor, next time you and Linny plan a surprise visit, don't. I'm surprised your mother let you. Not that I'm not tickled to death, you understand. Okay, everybody, move on out."

Chapter 9

➤ Hilary opened her eyes the next morning and saw tree shadows dancing on the ceiling. The sun was up and the soft summer breath from the open window next to her bed ruffled the curtains.

Her first drowsy thought was, Where am I? This small alarm chased away the sleepiness. She realized she was in her aunt's double bed in the back of the apartment. Aunt Josie had taken to sleeping mostly on the living room couch since her heart attack. It was her bed sometimes even when her husband was home. She claimed she didn't sleep well and wanted to be able to watch TV at all hours.

Hilary stretched her arms over her head and yawned and smiled up at the ceiling. She hadn't dreamed it all. Something funny had happened to Time, and the night before she was with her father again, not in Vermont with her mother.

Her mother! Hilary sat up straight with open mouth

and wide eyes. She had stayed out overnight and it hadn't even entered her mind to call home. Her mother didn't know where she was! She had to telephone her right away.

She jumped out of bed in such a hurry that she tripped over her sneaks on the floor. She staggered against the wall trying to keep her balance, and the thud woke Linny next door. He ran in, still half asleep, thinking it was his mother who had fallen. He had forgotten that she was out in the living room on the couch.

"You always sleep with your pants on?" was Hilary's distracted question. She was searching for her clothes, lifting the sheet, throwing the pillows on the floor, looking under the bed.

Linny picked up her shorts and tank top from the chair where they rested in plain sight, and sat down. He held her clothes out at arm's length, pinching his nose as if they stank. "You looking for these?"

"Was I? Well, never mind. Don't go 'way. I have to call my mom. Be right back."

True to her word, she was. "No answer. She's not home. Oh Linny, she doesn't know where we are!" She sat on the bed and looked to him for help.

He struggled to find something helpful to say but couldn't. He, too, had forgotten his Aunt Helen until this minute and could imagine how frantic she would be over their absence. He shrugged. "Nothing to do but just keep trying, that's all." A thought struck him. "Hey, Hilly, what are you going to tell her?"

This made them gape at one another and then laugh at their predicament.

"What do I say? Aunt Josie isn't dead anymore and sends her love?"

"Tell her Uncle Hal is home and still running around."

"Hey, cut it out, Linny!" She had told him about her visit with her father the night before and wasn't about to let him kid about it.

"How about I tell her we're fine, not to worry, and then hang up quick before she asks anything?" Hilary said. "I don't know what to tell her. What do you think?"

Linny shrugged. They fell silent for a long moment.

The room was so ordinary. The bed was rumpled, the faded blue-striped sheets in a tangle. The family pictures on the glass-topped dresser were of baby Linny and his healthy, happy parents. There was a crack in the beige plaster wall above the bed, and a closet full of clothes. Blowy curtains that needed a washing were at the window. The room was ordinary and familiar, yet they could have been on the moon the way they looked around, still overcome by the absolute strangeness of being there.

In a sudden spasm Linny closed his eyes and clenched the sheet. To be in his mother's old bedroom, knowing what had happened to her, was terrible for him. He thought to himself, Soon, so soon. Saturday is so close. She might die again, and I know about it now. I don't know what to do! His head twisted to the side and he cried aloud, "I can't go through it again!"

Hilary was frozen to the bed, knowing very well what he meant. She hadn't thought ahead that much. She had been so rooted in the present, so thrilled to be back when things were good, that the idea of losing it again hadn't occurred to her.

"When?" she whispered, following his thought. When would her Aunt Josie die?

"Saturday. Day after tomorrow. That was the date last year."

Still whispering, she said, "Do you think we can stop it, Linny? Stop it from happening this time?" Her hand rose to hold the ring, the way she would reach for a charm or knock on wood.

She had forgotten it wasn't there. "The ring! We have to find it, Linny." A fresh thought arose and tumbled out of her mouth. "Maybe the ring would stop it. I mean, the ring, like, got us here, didn't it? And maybe we have to find it so this time she won't, you know, die. I mean . . . Oh, I don't know what I mean." It sounded silly when she said it aloud, but it came from someplace inside, where it made sense.

Linny's legs twitched impatiently. His cousin's bug eyes and whisper and spooky air irritated him beyond measure. There was mystery here, certainly, something to be solved. It needed a cool head and logical thinking. She made it all so . . . fuzzy instead of sharp, dreamy instead of real. He couldn't stand that sloppy thinking right now. "Don't give me that voodoo stuff about the ring!" he cried. "It's my mother's life we're talking about!" He meant her death.

Then his resistance cracked. "Okay, okay," he said. "I'm sorry. I didn't mean that. It's only that I don't know what to think anymore. Sure, we'll look for it. Maybe it matters." If only the ring—or anything—could save his mother. He looked off, as if to the future, pain in his eyes, and fear too.

Hilary bit her lip and watched her suffering cousin for a few breaths. "Linny?" she finally ventured. "You know what? Today she's here. That's what you should think of. Isn't that a lot? Right now you can have breakfast with her. You know what I mean? Don't think of anything else. Come on, let's eat." She wished she could be more comfort to him. Eating always made her feel better.

Linny's mother had had a bad night. She had put heavy spots of rouge on her cheeks to cover the pasty skin, but all it did was make her look clownish. She was already in her chair watching the street when Linny and Hilary appeared.

She hadn't had breakfast yet. Linny went to the kitchen and returned with her tea and oat bran on a tray. She didn't want it. "I'm not hungry, thanks."

Linny found himself pestering her. She'd get sick if she didn't eat. He had never noticed what she ate before, but now it mattered. How did he know what might make a difference? Maybe if he had paid attention before, she wouldn't have gotten so sick. Maybe not getting her to eat was also his fault, his fault.

"Eat it, Ma," he urged, until she blew up.

"What's the matter with you?" she cried, her thin voice cracking with emotion. "All of a sudden you're pushing food at me. Hilly, what am I to make of my boy? A few days ago he didn't notice what I put in my mouth. I could have eaten this chair for all he noticed or cared."

Hilary was examining the jigsaw puzzle nearby. It was set up on the bridge table next to the chair. Since her aunt had gotten sick there was always a puzzle in the works.

She heard what Aunt Josie said and the way she said it. Hilly used to love being with her and Linny. Aunt Josie was the only mother she knew who would play jacks on the floor with them or think up endless card games on rainy days. She let them make a mess in the kitchen and didn't fuss, like that time with the peanut brittle. It had become a family joke. They had left it on the stove and it had boiled over, running all down the stove like a curtain of goo. They had to take turns, the three of them, breaking it up with the only hammer in the house. They'd say, "Chitty, chitty," and the one holding the hammer went bang, bang. A joke.

Hilly realized she hadn't heard Aunt Josie and Linny joke with one another for ages. Now Aunt Josie wasn't the same person. Sickness changes you, Hilly's mother had said. People who were sick couldn't think outside of themselves. Now, more than a year older, Hilly understood what her mother had meant. Aunt Josie wasn't thinking about Linny's feelings; she had room only for herself.

Josie leaned her head back and said, "Please, Linny, leave me alone. Go have your breakfast. Don't eat junk, have a banana."

"You want your jigsaw puzzle, Ma?" They had worked on it together the previous afternoon while Hilly was gone.

Josie opened her eyes and then closed them again. She was tired and it was still early morning.

Hilary waited through the hours for the phone to ring. Her father had promised to call. The sun rose higher, the clock ticked, and the phone remained mute.

Linny stayed on the sun porch with his mother. He kept watch on her breathing as she slept in the chair.

The need to search for the lost ring and their inability to do so made Hilary and Linny restless.

Hilary prowled around the apartment. Several times she called her father at the agency, but no one there knew his whereabouts. She tried him at home but no one answered. She told herself he had gotten tied up and couldn't get to a phone, and then she realized she was saying the very words he used to tell her mother when he didn't come home for supper. Well, so what. It was true then, and now too. He'd call any minute. She didn't let herself think about the strange woman he was with last night.

Linny longed for his computer back in Pittsburgh. His mother didn't even know how good he was at Nintendo. The music and lure of skateboard wheels reached him from the street. Eddie and Dopey Dan were out there practicing, and the sounds made his feet itch for his board. He should be out practicing for the tournament Saturday also, but there was no time.

He was held fast by his mother's breath. He went back and forth from his chair to the kitchen, from his chair to the bathroom, passing by Hilary, who sat near the phone without exchanging a word.

He couldn't leave his mother alone, and Hilly couldn't leave the phone. Yet the ring was on their minds and pulled at them like a beckoning finger.

For Hilly the ring was the magic that had transported

them on their backward journey. They had to find it, this solid token of the place and time they had come from. Without it they might be adrift in ways they couldn't know.

For Linny it wasn't so easy. Everything in him strained for logical explanations, yet he didn't have any. Ever since Hilary said the ring might stop what was ahead, it floated in his mind as enlarged as a life preserver on a ship. If only he could fit it around his mother and keep her safe! He told himself it was ridiculous, it was only a dumb ring, but he wanted it back with a passion.

They had a strong need to search for it, but the ties that kept them bound to the house were stronger.

The quiet of the morning was broken by a sudden commotion from the street. There were angry shouts, high-pitched screams and dog barks. Linny rushed to the window. His mother awoke and cried out, "What's that!" Hilary ran to the sun porch to see what was happening.

A little white furry dog ran alongside Eddie's skateboard, barking and nipping at it as if it were a live thing to bring to ground. Eddie was shouting at the little poodle, teasing it, luring it on, kicking it away when it got too close. Two small elderly ladies dressed exactly alike stood at the curb clinging to one another, screaming orders at the dog and at the boy. Neither the dog nor Eddie paid them the least attention.

At the window Josie chuckled and moaned at the sight. "Linny, go down. See if you can help. Those poor Munchkins! You have to save their awful Johnny for them. They positively dote on that dog."

Hilary laughed as Linny bounded away. "Munchkins, Aunt Josie? You mean it?" She had seen *The Wizard of Oz* on TV lots of times.

Hilary noticed that her aunt was breathing hard, as if she were short of breath. She wanted to help her back to her chair but her aunt waved her away.

"I just call them that." Josie giggled at herself like a schoolgirl. "They're . . ." She had to stop for breath. "You'll see," she gasped. She gestured with a hand. "Ask them up."

Meanwhile, down on the street, Linny had scooped up the little dog, who was furious at being taken from his archenemy, the wheels of Eddie's skateboard. He struggled in Linny's grasp, twisting to get at a chunk of flesh.

Eddie Gilberto wasn't all that pleased at being deprived of his fun. "Why don't you mind your own business, Erda. I'll get you for that!" He lifted his middle finger and shook his fist as he skated away.

Linny handed the dog to the two ladies on the sidewalk, holding it out at arm's length. He remembered the pooch as a bad-tempered animal, spoiled rotten by his mother's friends the Wightman twins.

"Why, Lionel Erda, Johnny and I thank you from the bottom of our hearts, don't we, sweet pea?" This was said to the dog by either Lenka or Rosa. He never could tell them apart.

The other one said to her sister with extreme irritation, "Give him to me, Lenka. You never did know how to hold him. He wouldn't have gotten free if I'd had my proper turn! And how is your dear mother, Lionel?"

At the window upstairs, Hilary needed to get their

attention. She didn't much care to yell out, "Hey, Munchkins!"

"Hey there!" she cried, playing it safe. All four looked up, including the dog. She waved and said, "Aunt Josie wants everybody to come on up."

At closer range Hilary saw why her aunt had named the two little people Munchkins. Rosa and Lenka Wightman were each about as tall as an average ten-year-old child. They wore identical white blouses and navy skirts as if they were on their way to a school with a strict dress code. They wore their hair parted on the side, chin-line short and held neatly tucked on the side by an old-fashioned bobby pin. Perhaps as a declaration of independence, one of them wore an unlikely sweatband around her head. The other carried a knitting bag over one arm and the little white dog in the other.

Linny led them to the sun porch and his mother. They stood in front of her chair and beamed at Josie, almost equal in height to the seated woman. Their features, like their bodies, had retained a kind of worn childishness, button nose, round cheeks. Only the deep crisscrossed lines on face and throat told the years. Certainly their lively eyes did not.

Chairs were drawn up. The Munchkin with the sweatband took Josie's hand in hers. "I declare, Josie Erda, you're a treat to see. I wanted to drop in yesterday when I was on my way to my Soup Kitchen. But Rosa warned me, didn't you, dearest?"

"I certainly didn't warn you! You say that just to annoy. I merely said you should call first. Josie might be resting." Rosa had taken out her knitting and was stabbing at the wool, which was much the same color as the dog sprawled across her lap, a dirty white.

Lenka checked her sweatband and said contentedly, "Rosa is jealous of my volunteer work. She carried on terribly when I gave a day for the homeless, didn't you, dearest? She wants me to stay home and be a stick-in-the-mud like her. Can you imagine me staying home?" She laughed at such a ludicrous idea and tossed her head proudly as if she were a teenager and her sister Rosa her crotchety old guardian.

The little dog suddenly jumped down from Rosa's lap and made a beeline for Linny, who was sitting on a wicker chair nearby. The dog had fallen in love with Linny's leg and began to show his affection. The embarrassed boy was doing his best to shake him off, but the dog had a good grip.

"Johnny, you bad boy! What are you doing!"

"Johnny, stop that! Come to mama, my darling."

This from both twins at full voice.

Hilary was convulsed. "Should I get some hot water?" she managed to ask.

A horrified "Oh, no!" from Lenka. "This comes over him once in a while. The vet says not to worry. Peanut butter seems to help. Do you have any?"

Linny was standing up, shaking his leg, but nothing discouraged the lovesick dog. He had a fleeting, almost forgotten urge to zap it, send the head across the room like old times. An even worse image entered his mind: The rest of the dog might just keep on doing what it was doing.

"Peanut butter?" Linny marveled.

"In a bowl," said Lenka.

"With a few crackers crumbled up," added Rosa. "He adores peanut butter."

The telephone rang and Hilary was off like a shot to answer it. When she heard her father's voice at the other end she couldn't help the cry that escaped her.

"Have you been waiting long? I'm sorry, princess. I feel like the lowest so-and-so, but hey, a man's gotta make a living, right? I got tied up here at work. You know how it is. As a matter of fact, this is what I'm calling about, sweetheart. I'm about swamped here."

Uh-oh, was Hilary's inward response to that. She could hardly hear him because of the noise on his end. Voices. Laughing, noisy, bunches of people. But she heard plainly that there was something coming she wouldn't like.

Her father said, "Okay, this is what's gonna be. I'm taking my best girl out on the town. How do you like that?"

Hilary's heart leaped. How wrong she was!

"Oh, Daddy! When?" she cried.

"What do you say to Saturday afternoon? It's only the day after tomorrow. Do I have to beat out a line of boyfriends, or do we have a date?"

"Saturday! That's so long! Can't it be . . . I don't know, why so long, why can't we . . . Saturday?" she wailed.

"Don't you think that's a little ungrateful, Hilly? Lots of girls would think tickets to the Ice Capades a treat."

"Ice Capades! Oh Daddy, I'm sorry. You know that's what I want most in the world. It's the best, most, well, that's the best!"

A memory tugged at her. Once before, they were supposed to go to the Ice Capades and didn't. She didn't remember the reason. What was it? And when? Whatever and whenever, this time it would be different. She would make it so.

"Daddy," she said firmly, "promise me that we are going to go to the Ice Capades on Saturday, okay? Promise."

"Hey, what is this?" She heard his full, surprised laugh. "You pinning me down here?"

"Promise me, Daddy."

"Okay, princess, I promise. We have a date. Now you stay right where you are, Hilly, with your aunt. With my hours I know your mother would want that. As a matter of fact I gave her a call last night, and she agreed that with my busy season you should stay with Aunt Josie. She said to give you her love."

Hilary said yes, yes, to the arrangement that he would pick her up Saturday at noon at their apartment. She heard him say that they could change into their fancy duds and drive in for the matinee. Her mind was on something else he had said.

Her father had said he had called her mother. He couldn't have. Her mother didn't know where she was, and certainly wouldn't have said for her to stay with her Aunt Josie, who was dead. At least she was dead in Vermont.

Hilary again dialed the number at the barn, and let it ring a dozen times before hanging up.

Linny found her standing in profound thought by the telephone as he came into the kitchen with Johnny for the peanut butter treat.

"What's the matter? You okay? Was that Uncle Hal?"
She nodded, too full to speak more.

As Linny prepared the bowl of peanut butter and crackers he told Hilary the news. "We can go look for the ring now. Rosa and Lenka are going to stay with Mom, and I got chased out."

The little dog ignored the treat. He had transferred his attentions from Linny to a dishcloth that had fallen on the floor. How he hated it! Hilary and Linny watched Johnny growl and snap at the cloth, lunging, tossing it up, catching it and lashing it back and forth.

They looked at this with some satisfaction and almost envy. The absurd little dog that looked like a dirty mop gone wild at least had a tangible enemy. If only they could grab events, or death, or disappointment in their teeth like that dishcloth.

"Come on," Linny said, taking Hilary by the hand. "Let's go find the ring."

"But where do we start?"

Chapter 10

Indeed, where to start? They had looked in the phone book under "Taylor Dilt," but there was no one listed there by that name.

They stood irresolutely outside the house, not knowing which direction to go. It didn't seem to make any difference which way. Walt Dilt had picked up the ring, they were fairly sure, and they had to find him. How do you find somebody who has disappeared? He was the needle, and the haystack he was buried in could be the whole of Brooklyn or, for all they knew, the entire cosmos. Walt hadn't said where he lived, but Hilary remembered knowing in a vague way that the Dilts used to live around there someplace.

She said to Linny, "Didn't I tell you something about them in Taylor's truck? Remember, when they were giving us a ride home from the deer? Back then? I mean, front then, if Vermont was next year." She giggled.

"What am I saying? Do you hear what's coming out of my mouth?"

Linny laughed with her. "Crazy. Back then in Vermont won't happen for another year. How's that again in English? Yeah, I remember you telling me something about them living around here, but that's about it. So think! Try to remember something else."

"I never paid attention since I couldn't stand either of them. I didn't want to admit it, but I hated that Taylor buttering up my mother." Hilary closed her eyes to focus her memory. "Wait a minute! He was doing the kitchen cabinets for the Sternliebs next door! That's how he met my mom." She broke out into her wide smile. "So, great! We ask the Sternliebs where he lives. We got 'em, Linny!"

But they hadn't. They hurried to Hilary's street and rang the Sternliebs' doorbell. When no one answered, Hilary recalled that they were teachers and had the summer off. They went traveling for the summer.

Once again they didn't know where to start.

"Come on," said Linny. "We can't just stand here. Let's just walk around, walk up to the avenue, walk the neighborhood. Maybe we'll see Walt. We've got nothing else to go on."

On the wide avenue, filled with stores, Linny was as excited and curious as a puppy on the loose. This was his old neighborhood and he hadn't seen it for a year. He was back and it was like putting on an old jacket he had loved and thought lost, or returning to a cozy room where he knew every crack in the ceiling.

He pulled Hilary to the lobby of the Oceana, the old

movie house, wanting to smell once again the familiar stale mixture of air conditioning and popcorn. He could see himself as a little kid, jumping with anticipation, waiting to shove his money at the lady in the booth on Saturday afternoons.

It came to him that he envied that boy, the boy he had been. How free he was then of what he carried around now, the terrible knowledge of how fast things could change. The kid he saw in his mind's eye was innocent. He didn't know what a chancy place his world was. One minute his life was fixed and usual; the next, what he took for granted was gone for good. And then you had to bear the memory of things you couldn't undo. Not fair! he cried to himself. I didn't know!

He stared blankly at the darkened lobby, lost in these thoughts. Hilary had to shake him out of his reverie.

A few doors away was Scotty's, the sport store. Part of the window display was a large poster advertising the prize skateboard that the store was donating to the contest on Saturday.

Linny stood transfixed in front of it, his forehead against the glass. Beneath the poster was a Zorlac Spider Metallica that he could kill for. It was upended so the painted spider under the board was visible. He saw the Deadbolt trucks and the Zombu wheels and he craved that skateboard more than the next breath. Some lucky kid was going to get it.

But he would be in that competition on Saturday! He could be that lucky kid. He had a good chance! He had worked hard enough at his tricks all the past year. He was good. At least he knew for sure that he was better than

Gilberto or Silverman, even if he hadn't touched a board in . . . what was it? He counted on his fingers, two days with his father, a day to get to the barn. They found the ring the day after that and yesterday morning they were zipped back here. Five days!

Only five days? It felt like five weeks! No wonder time could be fooled with. The clock could say one thing and the person who was living through that time could say another. Time was only fixed on the outside, not on the inside!

He held himself very quiet so as not to jostle the thought away, sensing that he was onto something. Time was truly a mystery. He thought of those long summers when he was a little kid, how they seemed to go on forever. Now summers were shorter. No, he corrected himself, they only seemed shorter. Two minutes at the dentist's could seem like a lifetime. Time could stretch or shrink, depending on who was living it and what a person was doing!

As he stared unseeing at the sport store's window and thinking of this, he became aware of a glimmer, a hint of an explanation for their being folded back in time. It was like the faintest of melodies, barely heard, but he was elated by it. There might be a logical explanation for their journey to yesteryear, after all!

He turned to Hilary to tell her about it, but something in her expression stopped him cold.

"What's the matter?" he asked.

"It's so queer to see this store here again. Scotty's went out of business, oh, ages ago, way back before Thanksgiving I think. I don't know why. It's a greeting-card store now. Isn't that weird? Now I know something nobody else does. It makes me feel all shivery. I'm like a fortune-teller."

"Well, as long as Scotty's is still here on Saturday giving prizes away." Linny told her about entering the contest as they walked along the busy street.

Hilary was only half listening. Linny was back to the neighborhood after an absence. But Hilary saw it all with different eyes because she was aware of the changes of the past year. He had been away, so he didn't know about them. She had stayed and knew things he didn't. For him it was all bittersweet joy. For her it was creepy.

They looked for the corn-colored hair and long bony face of Walt Dilt, hoping to spot him. They checked out everyone they saw. Strangers smiled back at them uncertainly, thinking perhaps they knew the boy and girl who were looking them over.

Hilary sang out, "Hey, congratulations, Mr. Cacciata!" to a rotund man leaning against the doorway of his shoe store.

He took the toothpick from his mouth and grinned. "Okay, what for? You gonna buy a pair of shoes someday?"

Hilary just waved and grinned back. She said to Linny, "He won the lottery last April, can you imagine? Piles and piles of money. First thing, he closed the store and went to Florida with his family. He doesn't know it and I do. I ought to tell him and make him faint."

The encounter cheered her. She passed a pregnant woman pushing a stroller, with two other youngsters toddling behind her like ducklings.

"Twins, Mrs. Steinham." Hilary waved as she passed by. Mrs. Steinham looked after Hilary with her mouth open. She clutched her belly and then laughed away the silly guess.

Hilary's grin left her as she passed a tall woman engrossed in conversation with a friend. She kept her eyes on the woman and nudged Linny. "See her? The one in the pink slacks? Her son got killed in the Persian Gulf this winter. Look at her laughing. She doesn't know. Maybe I should warn her, tell her to send her son to Canada or something."

Before she could decide what to do, someone hailed her. "Hey, Hilly! What are you doing here? I thought you were in Vermont!"

A girl in shorts with a pretty face and stubby legs smiled up at Hilary. She was with a boy Linny knew slightly from his old homeroom.

Hilary paled and cried out, "Roslyn!" as if seeing a ghost.

"Well, thanks a lot. Talk about being glad to see me!"

Hilary wasn't up to conversation. She gaped and said the girl's name again. "Roslyn."

"So how come you're home?" Roslyn gave Hilary a puzzled and uncomfortable glance.

Hilary managed to say, "Don't."

"Don't what?"

Hilary looked wildly at Linny and then plunged in. "You know your cousin Teddy? The one with the beer belly and motorcycle?"

"Teddy doesn't have a motorcycle. Beer belly, yes; motorcycle, no."

"Well, don't get on it!"

Roslyn laughed a gap-toothed gurgle. "This is a joke, right? Some kind of joke? I'm not to get on something my cousin Teddy doesn't have. Are you on something, Hilly? A controlled vegetable substance maybe?" She jabbed her boyfriend to share the joke. "I won't tell, honest I won't," said the girl. Still laughing, she moved away, leaving Hilary to stare after her, shaken to her toes.

Linny touched Hilary's arm. "Something happened to her?" he asked.

"An accident," said Hilary, tears starting down her cheeks. "She got killed. That girl I just spoke to got killed. Her cousin Teddy still can't walk. Our school had an assembly over it."

Linny started her walking again, but she didn't realize her legs were moving. Her mind was on her unknowing school friend. Roslyn was going to be in a terrible accident, only it hadn't happened yet. "She's not going to listen, is she? She's going to die and I know it."

Hilary halted and cried, "Oh, I hate this! I know what's going to happen, but I can't stop it! I don't like knowing the future! Not if you can't change anything. Walt isn't anyplace. We can't find the ring. I want to go home!" she wailed. She meant she wanted her mother.

She clung to Linny's two hands while streams of busy and indifferent people eddied around them. There was something else on Hilly's mind, stuck there like a thorn. She had to get it out into the open.

"Linny," she started, and then moved her lips over words she couldn't form.

"What? Come on, say. What?"

"Are we ever going to get back?" she blurted. "Back to where we were? Vermont? I mean now, get back our year?" She knew she couldn't say it right.

Linny knew exactly what his cousin meant. In the delirium of being back with his live mother he hadn't given return a thought. Now that he was prodded he was at a loss. He didn't know the answer to Hilary's question. He didn't know whether he wanted to return if he could.

Different feelings about it surged through him as he pondered, some of them hurtful. If he had to stay on and relive all that had happened in the last year, his mother's death and the time after that, then yes, with all his heart he wanted to return now. He couldn't bear to go through all that again.

The misery of those months and what it took for him to get used to his new life without her flashed across the screen of his mind like a fast-forwarded tape. A year of wrenching adjustment, filled with guilt and grief. A year of hearing her voice in his head, not having her, not leaving her. It was a year of knowing that he had loved and needed his mother more than he knew and, to his everlasting pain, more than she knew. Her dying with bad blood between them was like his walking around with an open wound that wouldn't heal.

He couldn't do it again. Wouldn't want to for anything.

But! If he could change things! If he could keep her from dying and go on living with her, knowing what he knew now, then no—he wouldn't return if he could.

"Well?!" Hilary was waiting for his answer. "It wasn't such a dumb thing to ask!" She pulled her hands away from his. She was insulted by his silence.

"Hey, no, no, I was only thinking. Honest. I don't know the answer, Hil. I don't know if we can get back our year. What I want to know is, can we change the things that have happened?"

They sighed and exchanged small wistful smiles and headed for home. They had given up on finding Walt Dilt for the day.

Chapter 11

When they returned, Linny rushed to lean over his mother's chair. She looked up at him with a kind of hectic gaiety. She had been entertained.

"I've been hearing about old times," she said. "The things these two remember! Tell them, Lenka, tell them about the ice."

The small woman was more than ready to be onstage. Lenka said to Linny, "Do me a favor, check that Johnny is still asleep in the kitchen. I think that bowl of peanut butter and crackers was too much heaven for him. Josie, if I were only thirty years younger that boy of yours would be in danger."

"Make that fifty years," said Rosa dryly.

The twins were side by side on a love seat opposite Josie's chair. Identical running shoes and white anklets hung halfway down. Rosa had her knitting. Lenka had the floor.

She said to Hilary, "Drag that thing over here, honey. You've got to hear this."

Hilary had gone to sit moodily on a wicker chair at the far end of the sun porch. She had a bad feeling about not finding Walt Dilt. The ring was gone. She wasn't in the mood for the scrappy old twins.

When Hilary reluctantly pulled her chair up, Lenka was ready. She looked to the ceiling in dreamy reminiscence.

"When we were little kids, the biggest treat was to follow the ice wagon down the street. This was before refrigerators, you understand. Nobody can believe I'm that old, but I can see it all as clear as clear."

"Hummph!" was Rosa's skeptical grunt.

"The iceman would cut a square of ice with his pick and hoist it with tongs to his shoulder, which was covered by a piece of tarp."

"Burlap," said Rosa, putting down her knitting for a moment so she could more fully enjoy correcting her sister. "It was a piece of burlap over his shoulder."

Rosa was talking to air. Lenka continued: "As soon as the iceman left his wagon to deliver his burden, we kids would grab the slivers of ice that were strewn on the floor of the wagon. I tell you, there was nothing better than following the ice wagon down the street on a hot day. The biggest treat in the world."

"No, it wasn't." This from complacent Rosa next to her.

Lenka bristled. "I declare, Rosa Wightman, I can't get a word out without you contradicting. You know what the trouble with you is? Jealousy, that's what. You know, sure as you're sitting there knitting those old rags of yours, that

I'm Johnny's favorite, not you. Who does he jump on first in the morning? Tell me that!"

Rosa was ready for battle, but Josie interrupted. She had always been direct. "You two are worse than a pair of three-year-olds. Why do you fight all the time? You know you can't get along without one another."

"Nor with one another!" sniffed Rosa.

Lenka said, "Well, if you know so much, what *was* the biggest treat in the world? If it wasn't the ice wagon, what was it?"

Rosa had her blood up. Her knitting was abandoned on her lap while she said emphatically, "You forget. You'd forget your head if it weren't sewed on."

Her explanation was for Josie. "The biggest treat for us was to save our nickels and dimes and go to Coney Island for the rings. You have to remember that was back then, when Coney Island was a showplace. Before it went downhill."

Now Lenka was beaming at her sister. "Oh Rosa, of course I remember. The merry-go-round. The brass ring!"

Linny slowly straightened from leaning over his mother. Hilary picked up her head and stared at Lenka.

Quietly Linny asked, "Brass ring? What do you mean?"

Rosa jumped in. "There was this enormous merry-go-round. And as you went around and around on your horse—and don't forget, it was fast, and going up and down too—you passed a kind of, what would you call it, Lenka?"

"I don't know how to describe it, dear heart. Arm, maybe?"

"Yes, let's say a wooden arm. One at a time, rings entered a slot at the end. When somebody grabbed one, another took its place. Most of the rings were made of, I don't know, steel maybe. Sort of nickel color. You have to picture it being at arm's length away from your horse as you passed it by. Well, you had to lean over, and if you were quick enough, you could grab one of these rings. But once in a while, instead of a steel ring there was a brass one. Looked penny color to me. Lenka here thought it looked like gold, wouldn't you know. Whoever was lucky enough to snatch that one got a free ride. The brass ring was a prize, all right."

Rosa paused and then barked a short laugh. "You can imagine how far Lenka and I had to lean out to reach the slot. Practically hanging by one foot. Remember, Lenka, our papa used to watch us from the bench with his arms uplifted as if to catch us?"

Lenka, all misty-eyed, patted her sister's hand.

"How big were they?" asked Hilary, afraid to hear the answer.

"The horses?"

"No, those rings."

"They were all the same size. I would say, like so," Rosa indicated, rounding her thumb and index finger. It looked to Hilly and Linny about the size of the ring they had lost.

"Were they bigger than what you could put on your finger, but not big enough for a bracelet?" Hilary hung on the answer.

"More like a shower-curtain ring?" prompted Linny.

Lenka positively beamed at them. "How sweet! It's so nice for young people to be interested in the past. That's right, Hilary dear. Too large for a finger, too small for a wrist. But I certainly wouldn't describe it as a shower-curtain ring!"

"I suppose the carousel must have had a lot of those brass rings," Linny said. "Boxfuls maybe." He was gazing fixedly at Hilary as he said this.

Lenka looked off into the distance wistfully. "I suppose. Of course they had to have a supply. But to me, getting that brass ring was like magic, the stuff of dreams." The child she was peeked out of her wrinkled face.

Rosa twitched impatiently. "Don't be such a damn fool, Lenka. Of course they looked exactly like shower-curtain rings. But you can probably see for yourselves if you want." She picked up her knitting.

"We can?" cried Hilary and Linny in chorus.

"I hear they are trying to upgrade Coney Island. I don't remember who told me, but they got the old merry-go-round running again, brass rings and all. That's most likely why I called it to mind. I must have told you that, Lenka."

"You certainly did not! You know I would have been down there in two seconds flat. Well, we'll pay it a visit sometime soon, dear heart. Won't it be fun? Oh, those brass rings!"

"How about tomorrow?" asked Hilary. The words just jumped out of her mouth, but her throat backed up with disappointment. She needed to find out for sure if the brass rings the twins were talking about were the same kind as the one she and Linny had lost. If they were, then theirs was just a common old ring after all, one of hundreds like it. She couldn't bear to find out that what she thought was a special magic ring was just another old-time gimmick for a merry-go-round.

The twins checked with one another by glance only.

"All right," granted Rosa. Then she took it back. "I don't like to leave Johnny alone. He gets mad at me when he's left alone in the house. I'll go some other time."

"He can stay with me," volunteered Josie. "He's good with me."

Lenka jumped down from the small sofa in order to take Josie's hand. "Thank you, dear one. Johnny will love that. I'm so sorry that you won't be with us. It will be such a pleasure to be with these young folk and see it all again through their eyes. You don't mind if we take them away?"

"But I'm not going!" declared Linny.

No amount of urging could make him change his mind. He glared at Hilary to warn her off. Tomorrow was Friday. He wasn't about to leave his mother on what could be her last full day, for what might turn out to have been an old door prize for a merry-go-round.

Hilary took him to the kitchen to plead with him.

"Look, you don't need me," he told her. "We have a second chance here, and I'm not lousing it up. I'm not leaving her, and that's that."

Hilary understood that well enough. Yet she gazed at Linny with big eyes, and her obvious disappointment made him add in a softer tone, "Hey, what's the big deal? All you have to do is go with the Munchkins and look at those old brass carousel rings. There must be piles of them. If our ring turns out to be identical to those billions of others, then I say, So much for magic. Our ring wouldn't be one-of-a-kind, but just something from an old merry-go-round, and nothing special. We can forget about it."

Impatiently Hilary said, "Okay, okay. And if our ring turns out to be different from the rest of those brass things, then what? If it turns out to be a one-and-only? Tell me, Linny. I want to hear you say it."

"All right, I'll say it. Then we will have to find it because . . . well, because maybe we need it, like you say. Hey, Hilly, you know I'm having a hard time with this. You're an easy believer and I'm not. I'm ready to say we need that ring and we don't know how to find it and we don't have much time. That good enough for you?"

It was arranged. Hilary and the Wightman twins were to take the subway for Coney Island mid-morning the next day.

Chapter 12

Hilary felt like a giraffe among Pygmies. It wasn't so bad when she was sitting across the aisle from the Wightman twins. The subway train was crowded even though it was ten-thirty on a Friday morning, way past rush hour. From the looks of the paraphernalia that people carried, they were mostly families on their way to the beach. Two lovebirds stood in front of Hilary, carrying on as if alone, hiding from view the two little people sitting across the way. There was no way to connect her with them.

It was when they came to their stop and got out at Stillwell Avenue that it struck her how funny the three of them must look together. She loomed over them as they walked along the street, one on either side, holding on to her hands like good children. From the rear the twins must have looked as if they were out for a walk with their nanny. From the front it was anybody's guess.

Rosa and Lenka were wearing the same school uniform

of the day before, navy pleated skirt and crisp white blouse. Hilary had a vision of their closet at home, a tidy line of blue skirts and white blouses. Which was a good idea, she decided. They wouldn't get into one of their fights over what to wear.

Lenka's only wardrobe problem would be deciding what to wear on her head. Instead of yesterday's sweatband she had wound above her bangs a red flowered scarf. The knot was at one ear and the ends made a cheerful splash as they fell across the white blouse.

Rosa was the navigator. She had written down the location of the merry-go-round and kept looking from paper to doorway and then back again, announcing each address as they passed.

Lenka leaned across Hilary to say to her sister, "Oh, do shut up, Rosa dear, and look around you. We know it's here on Surf Avenue someplace. We'll get there. Isn't it exciting to be in Coney Island again?"

Even Hilary, who was able to squeeze juice out of a stone, couldn't squeeze excitement out of the Coney Island she saw. The smell of tacos and hot dogs and pizza filled the air, thick as smog. As they walked along, rock music blasted from the souvenir, fast-food and video shops—Madonna mixed with Michael Jackson. It all seemed pretty ordinary to her. Maybe once upon a time it was great, but now it was no big deal.

Lenka cried, "Oh, look there!" She pointed across the street. "Nathan's!" She yipped as if she had spotted the Holy Grail. "Remember the hot dogs, Rosa?"

Surf Avenue was a wide thoroughfare with a constant flow of heavy traffic. For the moment a red light gave

them a clear view across the street and Hilary could see
the sign that had struck Lenka. It seemed to take up the
whole block, proclaiming NATHAN'S in letters that looked
to be as tall as a person. There were people lined up along
the open counter eating frankfurters piled with sauerkraut
even though it was still early.

"Are they good?"

"Good?!" exclaimed Lenka with a hand to her heart as
if struck in that vital organ. The red scarf dangling down
her blouse could have been splashes of blood. "Tell her,
Rosa." Lenka couldn't.

Rosa nodded at the restaurant across the street. "They
were good," she agreed. "Once upon a time. I haven't
had one in years."

"Let's have one right now!" cried her sister.

Hilary didn't want a frank. She wanted only to get to
the old carousel to see if her ring, her precious lost ring,
was the same as those others or different. She hoped it
would prove to be different; it would mean that she was
right, that the ring was special and unique and magic. All
she and Linny would have to do was find it again.

The way she saw things, the ring had gotten them there
and without it they might be in deep trouble. She knew
that from her terrible dream.

She had awakened Linny that morning before the sun
was up. She sat herself on the edge of his bed and shook
him until his eyes opened. Her hope was that he would
be able to talk her out of what had awakened her. It was
too scary to bear alone.

Linny had pushed himself up in the bed and groaned
as he looked at his watch. "You wake me up at five

106

o'clock in the morning to tell me a dream? Okay, okay, calm down. Go ahead. Don't mind me if I sleep through it."

She had tried not to show how scared she was, but she was never any good at hiding her feelings. "You have to listen to this, Lin. You know how a tape keeps playing the same thing, going 'round and 'round the loop if you don't stop it? It starts, and goes to the end, and then goes back to the beginning again? Well, in my dream that was us. We kept going through the same thing over and over again."

"It's too early for this, Hil. We kept going through what thing?"

"This whole year. I mean, I dreamed we got stuck living through this awful year over and over again. You know what I mean?"

"Where did it start? From, like, when we were born?"

"No, from the flood. We fell back to the time before Aunt Josie died, just like now, and then we had to go through all last year again with my Dad leaving and her dying and all the stuff after, right up to the flood again. Then we did the same thing, got on the bike, fell back a year, the whole bit. Over and over. It was horrible."

She managed to say this without having her voice tremble, but she knew she couldn't keep it up. "Linny, know what? It was because we lost the ring. If we can't find it again we won't move on. I know that from the dream. We won't be able to get out of the loop and just . . ." She stopped and swallowed.

Just live, she wanted to say. They needed to get on with their lives, grow up, grow old like everyone else. She

wanted to have boyfriends and kiss and go to parties late
at night and stay out if she wanted. She wanted to know
what her work would be, who her children were, who her
love would be. She always wondered when her life would
start, and maybe now she would never know. Without the
ring they would be stuck in Time.

There was a funny light in her cousin's eyes. Looking
at him she was reminded that she hadn't seen him blink
so much recently. He hitched himself up farther in the
bed and pulled his pillow up under his head. She knew
the signs. She was going to get a lecture, and she was ready
to listen. He would talk common sense and banish her
monsters.

He had his fingers ready to count off his points.

"First, in your dream my mom dies, and it isn't certain
yet that she will. Tomorrow's the day, and wild horses
won't drag me away from her. I'll be here, and this time
it's going to be different. Remember what I told you about
that last day? Our fight and both of us shouting and me
leaving? So if I can change that, maybe I can change
everything. See? She won't die! I'm not going to let her!"

Hilary could hardly look at him. His voice was charged,
his eyes blazing. She hadn't known that her cool, reserved
cousin could be so emotional.

"So already your dream is way off." He was calmer
now.

Linny ticked off another finger. "Two, a dream is a
dream, not a fact. There's a difference, Hilly, so don't
worry. We're not going to get caught in any loop. Your
dream doesn't mean anything."

He slid down in the bed and punched the pillow up.

Already he was drowsy. "You'll see. There's a carton full of brass rings wherever you're going with the Munchkins this morning. Maybe ours wasn't anything special, after all. Maybe there's a more logical explanation for how we got here. I have to think about it. Go back to bed, Hilly. Don't dream."

He hadn't helped her much, and as Hilary walked along the street with the Wightman twins recalling this conversation, everything in her rejected what he had said. In her mind she told her cousin, You can say my dream doesn't mean anything, all you want. I say we need to find the ring to leave the loop! And if our lost ring looks just like the others I see today, then, Linny Erda, we are lost too.

Since Hilary wasn't ready to sample a hot dog it was decided between the sisters that they would stop at Nathan's later for lunch to give the dear girl a treat.

They walked along and Rosa began to announce once again the numbers over the doorways they passed. Suddenly she stopped short and looked down at the paper in her hand. "Oh dear Lord, I'm so dumb I need a keeper. These numbers are going up! We are walking in the wrong direction!"

They retraced their steps, and as they hurried along in the opposite direction they began to hear the hurdy-gurdy music of a carousel.

It was a gorgeous thing, Hilary had to admit. Her two companions were outside having some kind of nostalgic fit. She had left them moaning and clutching one another at the entrance.

She circled the merry-go-round. The space in which it

was enclosed was painted an institutional green that had seen better days half a century before. But the carousel itself was a gilt and glittering circle of dashing horses that rose and lowered on poles. There were plush carriages that stayed fixed for the more faint of heart, and tamer horses near the center that didn't prance. But the pride of the stable were the beautiful flying steeds on the outer ring. Their manes were brown and wind-blown, their eyes bright and glossy. They were a show of bravery and spirit.

The tinny music howled out its good humor as cymbals crashed *bang-bang* with each note. The ride wasn't very crowded, and there were many solitary horses leaping on their poles. They passed Hilary with flashing eyes and permanent flying manes, each saying to her, You're not too old for me, no one ever is.

She saw a kid lean over and grab at something in the air as he passed. There it was, just as Rosa had described it! A wooden arm with a ring at the end. She looked around for the person in charge.

Lenka grasped her arm. "You see?" she cried with pride of ownership. "It's the same. Just as I remember it. Isn't it splendid?"

Rosa was with her, watching the spangled scene with a smile breaking across her face, giving light to it, changing her looks. Now she and her animated twin were identical. Only Lenka's scarf helped tell them apart.

"Let's ride," said Lenka to her sister, touching her shoulder, smiling at her, coaxing her.

Rosa didn't need coaxing. "I'm going to get the brass ring!"

Hilary declined their offer to treat her to a ride. She

went to find the person in charge. The merry-go-round had stopped but the hurdy-gurdy music continued loud as ever.

Hilary spotted a man lifting a child to one of the horses and passing a belt around her middle for safety. He was wearing a blue apron with a center pocket over his cut-offs. As he circled around, he collected tickets from the riders.

Hilary stepped up on the carousel and caught up with him just as it began moving again.

"Ticket?" said the man, holding out his hand. His bored face was made more doleful by a black moustache that drooped on either side of his mouth. He was looking around, checking the riders, hardly looking at her.

"I just want to ask you . . ."

"You gotta ticket?"

"Well, no, because I just . . ."

He held up a hand and shook his head, clearly annoyed. The merry-go-round was in full swing, and she had to shout over the music.

He indicated that she couldn't get off now. She was to hold on to a pole and wait until the merry-go-round slowed. He would get back to her. He was too busy for questions.

Hilary did as she was told but was burning with impatience. She looked around for the twins. They were both on outside horses, one behind the other. At that moment they were leaning out, almost falling off their horses in an effort to reach what was sticking out from the wooden post. Neither of them came even close.

For Hilary grabbing a ring was easy. She was a foot

taller than Lenka and Rosa, and had much longer arms. As she zipped by the post she reached up, hooked a finger in a ring and pulled it out.

It was one of the steel ones. It was very much like her own in size, but that was all. Again and again she passed the post always reaching a ring and always it turned out to be a steel one.

The carousel was slowing down, and so was Hilary's hope of getting the brass prize.

She became aware of shouts, angry ones, louder than the clanging music. The noise seemed to come from a part of the ride that Hilary couldn't see. The rounded center of the merry-go-round was a thick pillar of gilded carvings and mirrors. It was a fancy way of housing the gears and motors that drove the ride. From the other side of that, came the noise.

The carousel had slowed enough for Hilary to jump off. As it turned she saw two kids still on horses, screaming at one another.

"It's mine!"

"Finders keepers, it's mine!"

"Get outta here!" The first boy, about nine years old and a solid block of outrage, untied himself and slid down from his horse while the merry-go-round was still turning.

The man in charge saw this and called out a warning: "Stay where you are!" He swung toward him.

"He got my ring!" yelled the boy, ignoring the warning. "You let go! It's mine!"

Hilary, listening to them yell at one another, understood that one of the boys had grabbed a ring and couldn't hang on to it. Somehow the kid behind him managed to catch it on the fly. Nice going, she said to herself, amused.

The second boy cowered against his horse as the bigger boy went for him. When he saw that he didn't have a chance, he deliberately flung away what was in his hand.

An object rolled in front of Hilary. One of her feet moved of its own accord and covered it. Under her shoe was a brass ring.

Chapter 13

Nobody saw her.

The merry-go-round man was busy going from one horse to another, untying small children and lifting them down. Parents who had been waiting on the sidelines were now surging, collecting their children. Everyone was on the move. The two boys had gotten off and were still scuffling. In the general bustle no one noticed Hilary bend over, snatch up the ring and shove it in the pocket of her shorts.

The twins returned from their ride in a different mood from that when they began. Especially Lenka. All her ebullience was gone. She said to Hilary, "Dear girl, take my advice, don't get old." Even her red scarf drooped.

Rosa, at her side, snorted, "You think the alternative is better?"

Lenka ignored her. "I used to reach those rings when I was young. I did, yes I did! True, I was small, but limber. I used to hang off the side of that horse like a jockey.

Today those rings may as well have been in Timbuktu for all the chance I had of laying a finger on one. You, too, Rosa. I speak for both of us."

"Yes, sister, but the difference is, I'm not surprised. If you would act your age once in a while, it wouldn't come as any great shock."

That seemed to come as the last straw. Lenka looked at her sour twin with fat tears standing out in her eyes. She was so woebegone that Rosa patted her arm and said roughly, "Never mind that. We'll go and have a frankfurter across the street and you'll feel better. What about it, Hilary? Are you through here?"

Hilary had the bunch of steel rings to return and went to toss them in a box near the entrance. As she rejoined the twins her hand closed over the ring still in her pocket. She found herself reluctant to tell them about it, as if it had to be kept a secret. Everything connected to the ring seemed to call for secrecy. But she knew that made no sense at all. She had no idea whether what she had pocketed like a thief was the same kind of ring as her own or not. She didn't have the courage to look at it yet.

She forced herself to pull it out and show it to the twins. "Look what I found," she said, as if surprised.

Now she had a chance to examine it. Avidly she turned it over and over in her hand, hefting it, judging the weight, the color, the size. She wanted to smell it, to stick it in her mouth like a teething baby to get the feel of it.

What decided her was something other than the sight, the smell, the touch. This brass merry-go-round ring was not like the one she had lost, because hers said something to her and this one did not. Also, her own precious ring seemed heavier and thinner. She couldn't be absolutely sure, but she thought so. But what she was sure of was that when she first saw it in that abandoned house, there was an instant click of recognition. Her ring had said to her, Pick me up, I'm magic, I'm more than what you see. Now, as she inspected the one from the carousel, it was nothing. Just an old brass thing.

Relief and fear coursed through her. She was at once glad to be reassured hers was special, and fearful because it was still lost.

Still, doubt assailed her. Maybe it was just her imagination! She wanted to see a bunch of the rings together.

Lenka touched the ring with a finger and said with surprise, "What do you mean, you found this? This is the brass ring! Where on earth did you find it?"

"Right here. Honest. It rolled right under my foot."

Rosa was amused. "We break our necks for that and it lands under your foot. Well, go ahead. You get a free ride when you turn that in. We'll wait."

Hilary wasn't interested in a ride. She told the twins she would be right back, and went in search of the man with the apron. She figured he must have boxes and boxes of brass rings tucked away someplace. If she saw the lot, maybe it would chase any lingering doubt away. She would have something definite to tell Linny.

But maybe the man wouldn't show them to her. As she approached him a nice lie formed in her mind.

There was a lull to give people time to buy tickets. The apron man was busy talking to a heavily made-up woman inside the ticket booth.

Hilary put on her best smile and said, "Excuse me,

Mister. I owe you for a ride. Here, I found this ring on the floor, so we're even, okay?"

He glanced at her and nodded. He dropped the ring in his apron pocket and turned away. No smile, conversation over.

"Excuse me again, Mister. Can I ask you something? See, I have to write a report for summer school on the most interesting thing I did this summer. I'm going to write on this merry-go-round. It sure is interesting. So where do these brass things come from? I mean, do you have a whole bunch of them? Can I see them?"

She now had his attention. He grinned at her, showing some gaping holes in a mouthful of bad teeth. No wonder he didn't smile. Pleased, he stroked the black hairs that framed his mouth like parentheses. "A report, huh? I remember them things. So hey, you wanna take my picture? Only kidding, kid. Yeah, I got rings coming out of my ears. C'mon, I'll show you. Be right back, Wendy," he said to the lady in the booth.

On the floor behind the wooden arm of the carousel was a cardboard box filled with the coppery rings. Hilary saw immediately that they were all exactly alike and none of them was like hers. She dug her hands in the pile and lifted a few at random.

"Can I keep one?" she asked. She would show it to Linny so he could see for himself.

"Sure, but now you gotta pay for your ride." He smiled his awful smile and winked at her. "Only kidding, kid. Go ahead, take one. But make me nice in that report, you hear?"

When she looked for the Wightman twins they were

talking to the lady in the ticket booth. Their chins reached no higher than the ledge, and stout Wendy in the booth had to lean over to see them through the mesh screen.

Lenka was once again her rapturous self. She turned to Hilary and with hands clasped under her chin said, "We have just heard the most fascinating news! This nice lady has told us of a new museum that's starting up here in Coney Island. It's full of old times, full of memorabilia about this dear old place. Now isn't that the best idea you ever heard of?"

Hilary could think of several million better, but she smiled and told Lenka that was nice, sure, a great idea.

Wendy the ticket seller was having a good time with the twins. Her news had stirred up some welcome excitement. She touched her tightly permed hair with a pleased hand and smiled at them. Her bright red lips and gold tooth were a good match for the glittering carousel behind her. "Yeah, I'm telling you. They collected all kinds of old stuff, I hear. G'wan over and see it. It's only over by the boardwalk. You want, I'll find out if they're open. I don't think it's every day. Wait a sec."

She opened the side door and bawled, "Hey, Charlie, that place open by the boardwalk? The one with all the old crap? Excuse my French, ladies. You know what I mean, Charlie, Ziggie's place."

The apron man must have heard her even above the music, for she nodded and said to her audience, "It's open. Here, I'll write down where it's at. You go have yourselves a good time, you hear? My pleasure."

They stopped for lunch before hunting up the museum,

and Hilary had her promised hot dog at Nathan's. She hardly noticed the taste. Abstracted, she stabbed at the thick fries with the wooden spear. The couple leaning against the counter next to her, taking bites of each other's hot dogs, reminded her of her father and that lady he was with the other night, Mrs. Malkin.

Hilary felt as if she were split in two and both sides were arguing with one another. One side said, Forget the ring. Forget the loop. You are with your own daddy again, so stay with him. You have the chance to stop him from leaving this time. Linny had said this was a second chance. She could change the way things had turned out.

The other side of her said, What can you do? How can you change what happened? It was as if she had put on different glasses and they didn't fit her eyes. She was no longer able to see her father clearly. He had out-and-out lied to her, and it had never occurred to her that he would or could. So what else was she wrong about?

A French fry fell off her spear to the sidewalk, and Hilary used that to vent her feelings with an open cry. The twins were startled by her vehemence.

Lenka said, "Never mind, dear one, we'll get another order. You can have all you want."

Rosa, after an appraising glance at Hilary's flushed face, said to her sister, "You couldn't tell trouble if you tripped over it. What's the matter, child?"

"Nothing," said Hilary. A sharp need for her mother, a new look at her father, and a shiver of fear over the lost ring were more than she could explain.

A short time later they were on the boardwalk looking

up at a sign that said DOWN MEMORY LANE. Under it in script was written: *See Old Coney Island.* The museum shared a small single-story building with a T-shirt store.

"Not much of a museum," snorted Rosa.

She was right. The young man who took their money and parted the curtain for them to enter told them that the museum was just beginning to collect all the old stuff. There was lots more in the back not on display. So much of what the museum had was in storage, waiting to be restored. They should come back again next summer.

"Oh, we certainly will," Lenka assured him warmly.

Inside there wasn't much of interest to Hilary. She had to hide from the Munchkins her impatience to go home. Linny had to be shown the carousel ring, and maybe they could look some more for Walt Dilt. Not that she was optimistic. Somehow she had to accept the idea that their ring was lost.

The whole collection of memorabilia didn't take up the high-ceilinged yet small room. Down the middle, on a long wooden dais, sat an iron Steeplechase Park horse, and next to that was an age-blackened wicker push chair once used on the boardwalk. Beneath them was a blue Dodge-em car from old times, cordoned off lest someone was tempted to sit in it.

Hilary left the Wightman twins exclaiming over each object and wandered about the room looking at old snapshots of the once famous resort. Along one wall was a glass case that contained the remains of a creature about the size of Lenka or Rosa. It had claws and a tail. A sign on the bottom of the case said that it was a Fiji mermaid.

It looked so patently false that Hilary said to herself,

Sure, like I'm a creature from outer space. Then it occurred to her that she was a Time traveler and nobody would believe that either. Yet here she was. It had happened. There must be plenty of strange things that happen that people don't believe. You have to keep your mind open.

That idea cheered her up some. She even was able to smile at herself in the trick mirrors that showed her to be short and wide as a barrel. "An improvement," she said aloud.

The mirrors were next to a worn plaid curtain that separated the display room from the back. From someplace behind the curtain came the sound of hammering. Thinking that it was part of the museum, Hilary parted the curtain and entered.

It was murky in the room, the only light coming from a high window of yet another room on the far side. She stood where she was until her eyes adjusted to the dimness.

She could make out shapes, big clumps of objects strewn about. Shredded posters hung from the ceiling, disfigured Kewpie dolls leaned one against another along a shelf. A dented Cyclone car was upturned against the wall. There were carousel horses without paint, without legs or ears, some still upright, a few on the floor.

Hilary realized she was in the storeroom of the museum, like the waiting room of a hospital. Everything in it was old and broken and in need of the mending doctor.

She picked her way around the darkened room and came face to face with a towering monster. It moved. She screamed in terror at the sight.

121

The door of the far room opened. "Who's there!" cried a shape outlined in black against the light.

As he came toward her, Hilary realized two things at once. The towering monster was herself in a trick mirror against the wall. The other was that the man approaching her was Taylor Dilt.

Chapter 14

Relief, and a high swing of joy flooded through Hilary at the sight of Taylor Dilt. She cried out his name and flung her arms around him. He meant home and her mother. He meant finding Walt Dilt and the ring. His appearance was a shining moment of miracle to her. She was so terribly glad to see him.

"Whoa, Miss. Take it easy." Taylor grinned in his lopsided way at her. He reached up and pulled her arms away from his neck. "Was it you, screamed just now? You okay?" He didn't know her from Adam.

"Oh, Taylor," groaned Hilary happily. Of course he didn't know her. This was the year before he came to Vermont, a whole year before he came on to her mother and became Hilary's enemy. He hadn't met her yet. She was still a stranger to him.

" 'Taylor,' is it? How do you know my name? They mention me outside?"

It was too dim to see clearly, so she felt rather than saw

his amused, steady gaze, full of goodwill. Once again she had to improvise in a hurry.

She nodded and, hoping he wouldn't ask any further questions, said casually, "Yes, the ticket-booth man said you were back here. I need to ask you something." That last at least was the truth.

"Well, you certainly got my attention. You sure you're okay?"

She explained about the apparition in the mirror. He laughed and took her hand in his and headed for the lit room. As he expertly picked his way through the debris, he said over his shoulder, "They should really take down that curtain and put up a door. I don't tell them that because they probably would have me do it, and I'd rather stick with my wrecks. People wandering in here could bang themselves up real good on this junk. Their insurance won't cover, I bet. That, or get a light for this place. In you go."

She had never heard him say so much. It was clear that he was trying to put her at ease. He thought he was a strange man to her, and he didn't want her to be scared. The idea of being scared of old Taylor made her smile.

His workroom smelled of paint and wood shavings. It had the sharp metallic smell of nails and hinges and assorted hardware. Hilary breathed this in. She loved hardware stores. On his workbench a vise held in its grip the prancing leg of a merry-go-round horse. Above it was a long, hooded bank of fluorescent lights.

Taylor Dilt sat her down on a workstool and leaned against his bench with his arms crossed over his chest. "Okay, shoot. What can I do for you?"

124

Hilary leaned forward. "Do you know if your son Walt found a ring?" The blood drummed in her ears. So much rode on his answer.

Taylor repeated the word "ring" to the room and thought it over. His long face gave it serious attention but was blank until memory struck. He said with some surprise, "Oh, you mean that old carousel ring? That what you're talking about?"

"Yes, yes!"

"Well, I'll be. He told me he found it in the gutter someplace. Seemed like an odd place for it to be." Taylor regarded her with amusement and curiosity.

"It's mine! It's ours! Oh please, is Walt around? Where can I find him? I want my ring back!"

She was out of her seat, ready to leap away at his answer.

Taylor raised quizzical eyebrows at her. "It's not going to run away. It's safe with my boy. Sit. By the way, what's your name?"

Hilary told him. It felt so funny saying her name to someone who knew her so well, that she had to giggle.

"Now I have to ask you something. Why do you look at me that way?"

"What way?"

"Girl, you know very well what way. I noticed it right away. Like you know something I don't. Like you know something about me."

It was true she was looking at him with knowing eyes. It was fun to know so much about this man that he didn't dream of. He had no idea that he was going to move to Vermont and meet her mother and fall for her. What if she told him about landing here from another time, and what was in store for him? Would he think her crazy, or what?

She lowered her eyes, hiding them from him. She couldn't answer.

He tilted his head at her, smiling ruefully. "You kids. Never ask a question of kids. I should know better."

He went from his bench to a corner of the room where there stood a block of wood. He sat himself on the stool in front of it and, picking up a curved knife, began to work at it. Hilary rose to see what he was doing. Emerging from the wood was the face of a beautiful spirited horse.

She breathed rather than said, "Wow."

"I take it that's a compliment?" Taylor grinned. He stopped working on the horse to say, "Merry-go-round horses are a hobby of mine. As you can see." He pointed with his chin to the line of broken old steeds next to the workbench, waiting to be fixed.

Hilary recalled being with Linny and Walt in the back of the pickup truck after the accident with the deer. She could see a tarp covering a big mound and knew now that it was a piece of wood to be carved into one of Taylor's horses.

He pointed the curved tool at her and said, "About that ring of yours. Where did you get it? My son showed it to me because he thought it might belong to an old-time carousel like the one I service around the corner. Tell the truth, I thought so, too, at first, but it's not."

Hilly was rapturous. She clasped her hands together under her chin. "You don't think so either!"

"I know it's not," Taylor said. "That ring of yours is a

funny old thing. I get curious about old things." He laughed a little at himself and gestured once again around his workshop. Hilary thought it a wonderful place.

He bent over his carving once again but continued talking. "It's not valuable, you know, but it's interesting. So where did you get it?" He looked up expecting a straight answer.

She gave it to him. "My cousin and I found it in an abandoned house."

"You didn't scratch those marks inside it?"

No, she hadn't. She remembered the marks were there when they had found the ring, but she hadn't thought anything of it. Taylor seemed to find that the most interesting thing of all.

Faintly Hilary heard cries of her name. Her hand flew to her mouth. "I forgot!" The twins were looking for her. They had dropped completely from her mind.

Taylor said hurriedly, "You'll find Walt on the boardwalk near the ramp just a few yards right of here. He's on his skateboard. Go on. Your friends will think the mermaid ate you."

She laughed and was suddenly awkward and reluctant about saying good-bye to this man she had once thought was so awful. She wanted to do something, say something, give him a present.

Impulsively she took his hand and traced the lines of his palm with a finger. She intoned in a spooky voice, "Madame Shazzam, the greatest fortune-teller in the world, sees a tall, dark woman waiting for you in a far place. There's a big romance in your future." She didn't know how far to go, but she could leave him with this.

"Oh, yeah?" He was amused and wistful at the same time. "I can sure use a little of that, Madame Shazzam. What else you see besides a dirty hand?"

She was about to leave it at that, but was impelled to add one thing more. "Ooh, I see an obstacle to the romance, a daughter. I mean, a girl. I can't tell who she is, but she gives you trouble. But don't worry about her. She'll change." Hilary smiled into his friendly eyes and said it again. "She'll change."

"Very nice. I'll hang in there if Madame says so. Now I'll walk you to your friends."

On the other side of the curtain the twins were waiting. Hilary persuaded them to wait for her while she looked for Walt Dilt.

They found an empty bench on the boardwalk directly opposite the museum, where they could sit in the sun and look out over the turbulent beach and calm ocean.

Hilary ran off to find Walt, her eyes trying to take in all directions at once. There was no missing him. He was the only boy flipping up and down a concrete ramp that ran down from the boardwalk to a side street.

Hilary leaned against the rail and watched him for a moment, savoring the fact that he was there. She wished Linny were with her to share this end to their search.

Walt was totally absorbed, crouching and standing as he sped down the ramp onto the street. As he returned, with one foot on the board and the other pushing, Hilary called to him. "Hey, you. Walt. Hi!" She waved her arm, gesturing for him to come over.

He glanced at her blankly, raised a palm out of politeness and down he went again.

Hilary thought to herself, what nerve. He's so full of himself he can't bother to talk to me. Maybe he didn't remember her. According to him, he had just met her that once.

A feeling of being alien, out of her natural time period, washed over her, a wave of strangeness. It was a worse feeling than being homesick that one time she went away to camp. She shook it off and told herself at least she had been right about Taylor's son. She didn't like him before and she didn't like him now.

She was waiting for him at the top. "Hey, I want to talk to you. Don't you remember me? My cousin and I fell over you on our bike a couple of days ago. You were skateboarding on our block?"

He looked at her then, and recognition registered in his light eyes. He nodded with a "so what?" expression on his face.

"So your dad says you found our ring." She held out a hand. "Give it back!"

Walt was wearing heavy denim baggy shorts with black kneeguards. On his feet were black high-top sneakers, over his yellow hair was a black baseball cap with a white bill, over his chest, nothing but a gold chain. Hilary had to admit he looked great.

His hand went to his pocket and stopped. He hoisted up his board and said, "What ring?" Wrapping a hand around the grip tape, he walked off.

"Come on, Walt. Cut it out. I know you have it!" She was running by his side to keep up. Even though she was a little taller, he had a longer stride.

"'Zat so?"

"Hey, stop. Wait up!" This was getting ridiculous. He was walking away again.

When they were face to face, she said in a baffled way, "You don't talk much, do you?" He wasn't like other boys she knew.

"I talk. When I have something to say and someone decent to say it to."

She was about to flare out at him, when she saw from the lift of his lips that he was teasing her, having some fun. This took away all her steam. Simply and directly she said, "Please, Walt. Don't be like that. I really need that ring."

That did it. "Aha, I knew there must be a person inside there someplace, if I worked at it." He pulled out the ring and dangled it high over her head, again teasing. "This happen to be what you want?"

She lunged for it and the ring fell from his finger. It dropped to the boardwalk, rolled, then fell through a crack.

Hilary stared in utter disbelief at where it had disappeared. It was as if it had a mind of its own and had twisted away deliberately, not to be caught by her.

Walt saw the stricken look on her face and immediately was contrite. "I'm sorry! Don't worry, we'll find it. Tell you what. You stay here and don't move, so we know where it dropped. I'll go under, and if I don't see it right away you let me know where you are, okay? What's your name again?"

Hilary told him in a gasp. He ran to the ramp and skated down. It was the quickest way to get under the boardwalk.

As she waited, Hilary was finding it hard to breathe.

130

Maybe the ring didn't want them to find it. She had been so close, and now again, unbelievably, it was gone.

She heard her name called from someplace under her feet. It was Walt trying to locate her. She got on her knees and cried, "Here I am!" through the wooden boards.

"I got it!" Walt's triumphant voice came up through the slats. "Come on down."

It was spooky under the boardwalk, sunless and dingy. Above Hilary's head was the muffled tramp of footsteps, but down there was cold silence, like a waiting thing exhaling bad breath.

As she ran toward Walt she had to dodge dented soda cans and other scattered garbage. A chill rose from the sand to her knees and followed her like a tangible mist. In the shadows, and strewn around the pillars like litter, were sleeping homeless people, motionless as the dead. She saw other bodies, entwined, too absorbed to care if they were seen. It all smelled of damp sand and unlit air and decay. It was as if she had left all bustle and light behind and were now passing through some kind of dark, dead place. The back of her neck prickled. She hated it down there.

Walt stood waiting for her like a beacon of safety. He held out the ring, which seemed to glow in the gloom. She grabbed it and, when it was safely in her fist, clutched it to her heart.

Out of the shadows lurched a drunk in cutoff jeans and a filthy T-shirt, carrying a brown paper bag. He stumbled toward her and held out the bagged bottle. "Hey, baby, wanna drink?" His loose lips spread, shiny with spit. With a cry of revulsion Hilary sprinted away, out from under, out toward the brilliant beach, out to life and sunlight.

131

Walt caught up with her. They sank to the hot sand. He said nothing but sat quietly beside her until her panicked breathing slowed.

She unlocked her fingers, which had been clenched so tightly around the ring that her knuckles were white.

"It means a lot to you?" Walt asked, indicating the ring. He moved his hand along the nose of his skateboard as if in sympathy with someone liking a thing.

He nodded when she said yes, and left it at that when she gave no further explanation. He seemed to understand she didn't want to talk about it.

Hilary held her face to the sun, not having entirely shaken off the horrid place she had fled. She shivered, glad for Walt Dilt's friendly silence.

She felt his warm hand on her forearm steadying her. He looked at her then with his straight gray eyes and for an instant or two she held his gaze with her own. From the coursing of her blood she was aware that an exchange was taking place between them, a kind of liking new to her.

Lenka's hail split this silent bridge like an explosive charge. They looked up to see her leaning over the rail of the boardwalk and waving as if her ship were departing. "Dear girl! You had us frantic! Yes, you did, you did. Come at once. We must get home to Johnny."

Hilary jumped up and said to Walt, "I have to go. Thanks." She held up the ring. "I mean, thanks for everything."

"Will I see you again?" he asked.

He had no idea why that was so funny.

Chapter 15

The euphoria of the afternoon—finding the ring and, in more ways than one, finding Walt Dilt—lasted Hilary until after supper, when once again she tried to phone her mother in Vermont.

She knew her mother must be frantically searching for her. Hilary pictured her wandering back and forth to Stockville, calling out her name in vain. She saw her wearing an old shawl on her head, thin and suffering, sorry for every cross word she had ever said to her missing daughter. The vision brought enjoyable tears to Hilary's eyes.

She imagined Sheriff Coleman with his tracking dogs and big flashlight, combing the woods, beating the bushes, looking for her lifeless body. After all, she had been gone for three days. Her picture might be on milk cartons.

"How come I can't reach her, do you think, Linny? I let it ring and ring and ring, and she never answers."

"Maybe she's out having a great time with Taylor Dilt. Ever think of that?" They were in the kitchen doing the supper dishes. She rinsed; he put them in the dishwasher.

This stopped Hilary cold. "Don't be silly. I just saw him this afternoon!" Then she laughed a little and said ruefully, "Oh. I forgot." She must no longer think in the everyday, ordinary way.

She turned the water off and leaned her back against the sink. Her bottom lip caught between her teeth, and two folds of concentration appeared between her eyes. It was hard to find the right words for what she wanted to ask.

For a moment she watched her orderly cousin fiddle with the dishes, lining them up just so in the dishwasher. She would have tossed them in like paper in a wastebasket. Finally she said, "I just can't get it through my head, Linny. Is our real life, I mean the one we left in Vermont, still going on while we're back here? You know what I mean? Is Walt here or there? Which Walt is real?"

She kicked the baseboard she was so confused and frustrated. "I don't know how to think about these things!" She had been with Walt Dilt that same afternoon. How could he be in Vermont at the same time? Why couldn't she get through to her mother?

Linny had been thinking along these lines since the glint of an idea had floated into his mind the day before. He now had some kind of an answer for Hilary—and for himself.

It had come to him that very afternoon. He was watching his mother nap on her couch and wondering what to do with himself. It was so quiet in the house he could hear the clock ticking in the kitchen. Hilary was at Coney Island with the Munchkins, the TV would wake his mother, and the books in his room were too young for him now. What he longed for at that moment was his computer. He could see it sitting on his desk in Pittsburgh, waiting for him. The screen would be blank. Nothing in the workspace. He thought about what he wanted to put in the workspace, and that's when the answer came to him. The logical explanation.

But knowing something in his head was different from saying it out loud. Especially when it came to explaining it to his cousin. She would more readily swallow the idea of leprechauns than what he was about to say.

He sat her down at the kitchen table and took a napkin from the holder to draw on. "Now just hear me out, okay? I know you're going to say it's crazy, but it's the only thing that makes sense to me."

"More sense than this?" She couldn't keep her hands off it: the ring once again was around her neck and she flashed it at him. When she had returned from Coney Island and told him all about her triumphant afternoon, Linny had tied it back on the shoelace.

"Lots more sense."

His mother called out from the dining room, "What's taking you two so long in there? I'll be waiting out on the porch, Hilly." If her energy lasted, she was going to fix the hem on Hilary's one and only summer dress so the child could wear it the next day when she went to the Ice Capades with her father.

"I'll be right there, Aunt Josie."

Linny started drawing on the napkin. "This is us going

along on this straight line. Think of the line as time, and here we are on it. I mean, we were on it; we're not on it now. I'm going to call that 'Time World One.' Okay so far?"

"Sure, Captain Kirk. Time World One."

"Okay now, here's another line." He drew another straight line beneath the first. He stopped before they were of equal length. "Hilary, maybe there's another Time World. Same as ours. That's this line here. I'll call this line 'Time World Two.' See, this one goes along its own track just a little behind Time World One. You with me so far?"

Hilary had to laugh at how serious he was. "Sci fi stuff, right? I get it. You're always reading that stuff. So what?"

He plunged on. If he stopped to argue with her he'd get all mixed up. "Okay now, think of these two Time Worlds like two files in a computer memory," he said. "This file"—he pointed his pencil to the first line— "that's us in Vermont. That's what we always thought was the one and only track there was for time."

What he said next made his own scalp prickle. "That's the one we were on when we slipped."

Hilary's mouth made an O.

"Yeah, we slipped." He started to speak, but then stopped and shook his head at her. "I wish you knew more about computers. This would be easier."

Linny hitched his chair up closer and pointed to the second track he had drawn. "See, this file is behind the first. It's running a whole year behind. And that's where we are now. We slipped a file. Glitches happen in computers, why not to us?" He tossed down the pencil as if he had proven a point. It was a great comfort to him to have discovered this explanation.

Hilary stared at him blankly. "Lionel Erda, you're telling me we sort of fell or slipped in like a time warp? And it goes along with the same people in it and all, only it's a year behind us? The same world, only it's running a little late, like a train?"

The way she put it was humiliating. "If you had any brains you'd understand! That's why you can't phone your mother. It's like any word processor. She's in a completely different file. She's stored in the memory, and we now are only on the screen. Where we are this minute, back a year, is only in the workspace."

He saw how she was taking this and pushed his chair away, exasperated. "You explain it, then. Go ahead. You have a better explanation? I suppose you're going to say that ring got us here. How? Where's the logic in that?"

Hilary clutched the ring. He had left out the most important part. The mystery of it, the magic. "A glitch!" she said scornfully. "It sounds like some kind of skin disease. Why do you always have to have logic?"

"Because that's what separates us from animals, that's why! With you everything is fantasyland. Why do you always have to dream up stuff?"

Hilary grabbed the napkin he was drawing on and tore it up. "Because that's what separates us from animals, that's why!" That should do him.

She stalked out of the kitchen, out to the sun porch, to her aunt.

Josie was resting her head against the back of her chair with her eyes closed. When her niece was beside her she sat up with an effort that Hilary didn't notice, and put on a show of animation. "Now where's that dress? Put it on, Hilly, and go get my sewing things in that middle drawer there." She pointed to a spindly secretary desk against the wall.

"You're sure I have to wear that thing?" Hilary asked for the tenth time. It was her green linen best. She put it on feeling like an overdressed stork, having grown a few inches in the past year. It was too short, and her legs seemed to go on forever, but her aunt didn't notice. Josie was adamant that she wear it.

"You want to look nice for your father?"

"Sure. Of course."

"Well, for once you can wear a dress. You want to make him proud. You'll be eleven next month. That's almost a young lady. Stop fidgeting, Hilly!"

"Twelve, Aunt Josie," corrected Hilary, whose mind was elsewhere.

Linny had come in and was leaning against the door frame. He saw the puzzlement on his mother's face and jumped right in. "Lying about your age already, Hilly? Maybe you can get away with it with other people, but I got news for you, kid. We know how old you are, don't we, Mom?" He shot a warning glance at his cousin, who rolled her eyes up to heaven and shrugged in apology.

His mother smiled wanly and said to Hilary, "What's that thing around your neck? I don't remember seeing that funny old ring on you before. Take it off, dear, that shoelace is a disgrace."

"I want to wear it, Aunt Josie. Look, it's beautiful."

"Well, if you really want it. Actually, it won't look too

bad on this dress, but take that shoelace off. Linny, in the top drawer in my bedroom is a long white box from Ming's. Bring it here, please."

Inside the box, Josie kept a collection of colored ribbons and silk chains. She chose a twisted length of purple silk cord and held it up to Hilly. "You like this? I think it will go nicely with that green."

Josie had Linny tie the ring to the cord, and Hilary slipped it around her neck, letting the purple cord show against the green of her dress.

Linny said to them, "Okay with you if I go out for a while? Maybe I'll go over to the schoolyard."

He couldn't wait to get to the schoolyard. After so many hours of being with his mother, he was so bored and irritated he could have screamed. He just couldn't help himself, even with all he knew.

Now that Hilary was with his mother he could take another look at the contest layout for the next day. He had watched it being set up that afternoon when he had taken his mother for a walk after she had awakened from her nap. It was a painfully slow walk, and they didn't stay at the schoolyard for long. He was dying to check it out again. He had to plan his moves for the contest.

Hilary was standing on a stool, revolving in front of her seated aunt. Josie had her mouth full of pins and could only wave her hand at him to say, Go, go.

After he left, Josie removed the pins from her mouth and dropped her hands in her lap. She looked up at her niece and said, with a humorous twist to her lips, "I don't know what's come over that boy. He doesn't leave me alone to breathe. Last week he couldn't get away from me fast enough. And now? The past few days I'm lucky to be able to go to the bathroom by myself."

She shook her head, perplexed and yet amused. "I know my boy. After five minutes he's itching to get away. Not that I can blame him. I'd like to get away from me, too, I'm such a pain in the neck these days."

Josie turned her head away and looked without seeing out the sun porch windows. "My poor boy . . ." She looked up at her niece, whose eyes were bright and whose cheeks were flushed with health. "I tell him to go, but he stays. Tell me the truth, Hilly, is something going on that you're keeping from me?"

Hilary couldn't bear this conversation. She stooped, and as she held her aunt's thin shoulders, she cried, "Oh, Aunt Josie, we missed you so mu—!"

She was quick to put a hand over her mouth. This was the second time she had almost told. Resisting the temptation to continue, to unburden herself to her aunt, was like fighting a strong current. She longed to tell Josie everything. She longed to have someone whom she knew and who loved her stroke her hair and tell her that everything would be all right.

But she couldn't tell her Aunt Josie that she had died and was about to die again. That Hilly couldn't do. She had to shut her big mouth and keep to herself that knowledge and everything else that had happened.

She managed to laugh it off and say, "It must be that skateboard contest tomorrow. It's on his mind."

Meanwhile Linny had taken the skateboard he had borrowed from Danny Silverman, a double-edge small with a tail but no nose. It was all right but old. The wheels could have been better.

He rode it to the schoolyard in the twilight, testing it with ollies off and onto the curb. It was good to feel a board under his feet once again, and he was reassured that he hadn't lost his touch.

The streetlights were beginning to come on, and when Linny got to the yard it was almost too dark to see. He leaned on the chain fence and made out the shapes of the course he was to follow the next day. He wanted that first prize skateboard so much he could almost taste it. A Zorlac was beyond his dreams. If he won it he could buy some skate rags and decals with his saved-up money.

The course wasn't bad. At a skatepark in Pittsburgh he had watched a tournament that scared him even to look at it was so tough. Since this one was for all ages and for intermediate boarders as well as advanced, it seemed very doable to Linny. The concrete of the schoolyard was in good shape, no crumbles that he could make out, but of course it was fairly dark now. He could make out the sets of triangular boxes with a half-inch rail along the top. They were short and low. He couldn't see how many jump-overs there were, but they were also low. He would have to kick out over a flight of six stairs. So far he could do it. What worried him was the wooden wall that had been put up for the contest. He judged it to be at least eight feet high, and lethal. He would have to set himself up with a lot of speed and then somehow ride straight up the sucker, turn himself around and come down on his board in one piece. He put himself on the board and planned with his body what to do, knowing how it should feel if done right.

He leaned his back against the fence and looked up at the sky. His mind turned to the next day, Saturday. The contest went out of his mind. Tomorrow loomed for a different reason.

Dread formed inside him about the coming day. It was a ball of fear that weighed down his breathing. On the same date last year, he had stormed out of the house the way he had done so many times before. He was in a sweat to get away from her and her sickness, and she knew it. There was that look in her eye. He wasn't a good son. She had no use for him.

Linny groaned aloud at this memory. He had never seen her again, and never thought to except in dreams. She had left him holding this bag of rage and self-reproach and grief. Until three days ago. He had slipped back to when she had yet to die and he had another chance to set it right.

But what to do? How could he save her? One thing, tomorrow he would not leave her alone for a minute. Not a single, solitary minute. Maybe that would make all the difference. If you change one thing, maybe everything changes.

Linny searched the sky for stars. The moon had risen but was blurred by strips of ragged clouds racing across its face. There were no stars. But the forecast on TV had said it would be sunny and clear tomorrow. That was a good sign. Last year it had started to rain in the afternoon.

He pictured walking with his mother to this schoolyard with a folding chair under one arm and his skateboard under the other. He would set her down in a good place. He must remember to bring an umbrella to shade her from possible sun. She would see what he could do.

He would see her pleasure and her slow smile, and he would keep her safe with him.

Chapter 16

"Let me wear it today, okay? Maybe it will bring me luck." He meant the ring that hung from Hilary's neck on its purple cord.

"Hey, look at you. You're doing that eye thing again, Linny. Stop blinking like that."

"I am? Well, I can't help it. Don't you think I have something to be nervous about?"

The fateful Saturday had begun with a shifty sun that soon abandoned the sky to a steady gloom—not rainy, not fair. The humidity was oppressive and made it hard to take a deep breath. That and the heavy anticipation of the coming day made them snap at one another.

It was mid-morning. Hilary was sitting on the edge of Linny's bed watching him dress for the contest. She knew why his eyes blinked and why he couldn't sit still and why he was getting dressed so early. He had a lot to worry about, and she had this great day ahead with her father.

Of the two of them, he should have the ring, but still it was a sacrifice for her.

She lifted the cord from her neck. "I don't know why I'm so good to you. Why do you want it? I thought it didn't mean anything to you. I was going to wear it to the Ice Capades today."

She held the ring out to him by Aunt Josie's purple cord. In the gray of the bedroom, with the shades still down, it gleamed. "Look," she said, admiring it. "Just like gold. I shined it up with some brass polish from under the sink."

Linny watched it swing from her hand like a pendulum, a center of light in the dim room. There was no way to explain the pull it had for him that his thinking mind rejected. He was drawn to it when he first saw it in the abandoned house, and was even more so now. The sight of it gave him strange comfort for the day that loomed ahead.

To Hilly he said dryly, "It does mean something to me. I used to have a rabbit's foot for luck."

He took it from her and put it around his neck inside his shirt and patted it. "I need all the luck I can get today." He meant getting through the day, his mother alive, the contest won. He meant undoing this time what had happened last time.

Hilary remembered something. "Hey, wait a minute." She ran back to her bedroom and returned with the brass ring from the carousel. She had entirely forgotten it since she had her own ring back. "Why don't you wear this one instead?"

"Sure. Why don't you?"

"Well, what should we do with it?" asked Hilly, setting it on her palm. It didn't mean a thing to her.

Linny shrugged, not having an opinion.

"I know what!" Hilary cried. "Let's give it to the twins. Can't you see them fighting over it?" For the first time that morning she was able to draw a laugh from Linny. He was busy giving himself a very dissatisfied once-over in the mirror above the bureau. He wasn't really wearing what he would have liked to wear for an important skateboard tournament, but it would have to do.

He had put on the same shirt, blue jeans and sneakers he had worn since he arrived. Nothing else fit him. He threw the clothes in the washing machine at night and put them back on in the morning. Nobody, including his mother, seemed to notice that he had grown a few inches in the year since he had worn the clothes in his closet. The only thing he had found to wear that would be useful for the contest was a pair of leather gloves. They would give him some protection that afternoon. He could borrow whatever else he needed from some of the other contestants.

"What time is it?" he asked Hilary.

"Same time as it was five minutes ago, only five minutes later. Take it easy, Linny. It's only ten-twenty in the morning. You've got hours yet. I'm the one who has to get to my house by noon for my date!" She giggled and tried to stop herself, and then erupted again.

The anticipation of the day with her father was spilling all over the room. Linny glanced at his cousin and envied her, but he was also a bit hurt. She could beam in on one thing and let the terrible rest go. Her skin was flushed and her eyes sparkled and her hair seemed frizzier than usual. She was electric with what lay ahead. How could she be so forgetful of what this day meant to him, of what might happen once again?

Hilary saw the way he was looking at her. "Linny, now you're making me nervous. Can't you think of it as just another day? It could be." She jumped from the bed. "I'm going to take my dress and my bike and go on home. Daddy said I should be ready by noon, but maybe today he'll be early."

She bounced to the door and turned, the smile gone. Impulsively she ran back to Linny. Nearly knocking him over, she kissed him quickly on the cheek. "Good luck today," she said. "I'm going to ask Daddy if we can have dinner here tonight. So we'll all be together, the four of us—Aunt Josie, Daddy, you and me. You'll see, it'll happen. Let me touch the ring for that. Let's both make a wish."

Without any hesitation Linny fished it out, and they rubbed their fingers across it.

Hilary collected her things and went out to the sun porch, where her Aunt Josie was at the jigsaw-puzzle table holding one of the pieces and gazing off into space.

Hilary leaned unnoticed in the doorway. There were purple smudges under her aunt's eyes and she seemed even paler than usual. Her dark eyes were unfocused, infinitely sad and brooding. She was wrapped in stillness, separated by her thoughts as if behind glass.

The girl withdrew for a moment and then stomped loudly back into the room. She was big and bright and her eagerness shook the corners. Josie, brought back so suddenly from her far shore, tried to muster a smile. She took a deep breath as if to take in the vibrant life of her niece.

"Hey, Aunt Josie, I'm going to go now, okay? I know it's early, but I want plenty of time to get ready. Is it okay if I ask Daddy if we can have supper here tonight with you guys? We can send out for Chinese. Give Linny a yell for me this afternoon. I want to hear all about it."

"I'm not sure I'm up to that outing today," Josie said. "A contest, is it? Linny is insisting I go. No matter. The boy doesn't need me there."

"He does! He does need you there! Oh Aunt Josie, you've got to go! Promise you'll try."

"Never mind. You go have a wonderful time today, Hilly."

"Oh, I will! Promise, promise you'll try to watch Linny today?"

Josie turned her haunted eyes up to the girl. "You think this means something to him?"

"I know it does!"

"Well then, I promise." She shooed her niece away. "Go on, get. Just looking at you tires me out."

Hilary stooped and clasped her aunt, shocked by the bony feel of her. "Bye, Aunt Josie. Take care, okay? You do that. See you later."

Hilary left the house with some relief. Linny and his mother had drawn a shade over her pleasure in this day, and now it was lifted.

She ran to the Munchkins' house a few doors down and left the brass ring in their mailbox. They would think it a gift from heaven. She imagined Lenka wearing it on her headband and Rosa squawking about her foolishness.

Hilary folded her good dress and her poncho in the basket of the bike that had been stored and waiting for her downstairs inside the entrance. She hopped on and set off for home, thinking with lively joy of the afternoon ahead with her father, all else forgotten.

When Josie made that promise she had meant it. She tried to conserve her energy, remaining quietly in her chair, not even doing her puzzle.

Linny gathered all that he wanted to take to the schoolyard and stowed it by the door—folding chair, umbrella, Thermos of iced tea, skateboard, gloves—ready to go. No helmet. He would have to borrow that from one of the other guys at the yard.

From the street he heard his name called. "Erda. Hey, Erda."

Linny stuck his head out of the sun porch window. It was Eddie Gilberto with a Spitfire tucked under his arm, a real beauty.

Eddie held up the skateboard. "Eatcha heart out. I just got it, and been breakin' it in all morning. You gonna come on over and see me win that Zorlac?"

"Nope. You got it wrong. I'm winning that skateboard, Eddie."

Linny could see surprise strike the face of the boy downstairs. "You?" Eddie said. "I didn't know you signed up. You don't even have a board."

"Sure I do. Danny lent me his old one."

"He did? That stupe! I'll get him. Hey, I know that board. It's no good." Then came amusement. "Anyway, I seen you skate. My sister Lorene could do better and she's still in diapers."

Linny was goaded beyond endurance. He wanted to wipe that smirk off Eddie's face for good and all. "Want to bet on it?" he said. "I bet my . . ." He hesitated and his thoughts raced. What did he have that Eddie might want? His temper up, Linny pulled out the ring from under his shirt and let it hang out of the window, swinging from the purple cord. It shone like the real thing. "I bet this solid-gold ring against that Spitfire that I beat you this afternoon. What do you say, is it a bet?" He wasn't risking a thing. No question he could beat Eddie.

"Yeah? You kidding me? A gold ring? Real gold? I knew you were nuts, Erda. Sure, it's a bet, sucker. Like I said, I seen you skate."

That done, Linny now had more butterflies in his stomach than before. It was a safe bet, but Eddie was right. Linny was crazy to be betting the ring. It was done, however.

He checked the clock in the kitchen. Ten past noon, time to take his mother to the schoolyard.

At the door she asked for her sweater, even though the day was a sticky one. Linny found it by her chair and bunched it to his nose to draw the odor deep inside him. It was what she had on that last day, when she was supposed to have died. Was that a dream? Was this?

He helped her on with the sweater carefully, making sure her thin arms didn't have to twist.

"Do I have my pills?" she asked for the fifth time. He

checked again to satisfy her. They were still safe in her purse. He would carry it for her.

So far so good. He hadn't lost his temper once. He hadn't slammed the door and left her alone. Things were different this time, as Hilary had said. The butterflies in his stomach began to settle down.

Josie stood for a moment at the top of the stairs. She took a breath and, holding on to the banister, stepped down. She sagged under her own weight. Linny was there to hold her up.

"I can't," she murmured. "It's not a good day for me, my son. You go on. I'll be fine here."

Linny pleaded, "No, no, I'm not going without you! Try, Mom. Please. I'll take you down. Maybe the fresh air will make you feel better."

His mother saw his need and, perplexed, for his sake said, "I'll try."

But by the time they reached the bottom of the stairs, it was clear that she could not go any farther. She would not be able to get to the schoolyard that day.

It wasn't anything serious, she assured him. It was just her stupid old heart acting up again. She'd be better off at home. "Go, Linny, do me a favor and go. Stop pestering me. Last week you were moaning about losing your balance on that skate thing. So what's so important that I watch you now? Both of you, you and Hilary . . ." She couldn't finish. She had no breath for this conversation. "Take me back upstairs."

She glanced around, her face shadowed. Her eyes met his. And there it was, the look that had haunted him for the past year! It was the very same expression that all this while he had thought held blame or anger or, worse, rejection. But now, a year older, no, a hundred years older, he was able to see it for what it was. It didn't have anything to do with him at all. What he saw in his mother's eyes was fear.

Linny groaned and in a swift movement picked her up and carried her back to her chair on the sun porch.

He looked at his watch. Almost one o'clock. Ten minutes until contest time.

The prize skateboard hung in his mind's eye like a star. Eddie's Spitfire was under his feet. All Linny had to do was show up. He knew those lonely months of practice in Pittsburgh would pay off. He knew he was that good.

But if he couldn't take her, he wouldn't leave her. He said good-bye to the contest, good-bye to the prize skateboard, good-bye to the Spitfire.

He had gambled away the precious ring. Now he had to forfeit it. He said good-bye to the ring; it was now Eddie's.

What was hardest to give up was the image he had of his mother's surprise at what he could do. Her smile, her pride in him. Saying good-bye to that made him groan as if he had been punched.

Linny walked to the window and looked down absently at the street, trying to absorb the unexpected turn of events. One of Silverman's cones was still against the curb. The sight of it made an idea jump into Linny's mind. He didn't have to say good-bye to everything! There was still something to be salvaged, something he could give his mother.

She was sitting in her chair with her eyes closed. He

gently shook her arm to get her attention. He wanted her to know that he was pushing her chair close to the window. "You sit there, Mom."

He ran downstairs with his skateboard. He knew that Dumb Danny had a stack of cones under a tarp in his backyard. Linny brought them out two at a time, running back and forth from Danny's backyard to the street. Then he set all twelve of them in a straight line just a few feet apart from each other, not far from the curb so cars could get by. On a Saturday there should be few cars to interfere, and Linny was so intent he wouldn't notice if they ran him over.

He waved to his mother to make sure her attention was on him, and then set down his board at a distance from the first cone. Getting up speed, he wove in and out of the orange cones like a skier racing down a slalom, shifting his weight from one side to the other without coming even near to knocking over any of the cones.

That was to get started. He looked up to his mother, who was now standing at the window.

He walked back to the start and again set his board at a distance from the first cone. He lifted his chin to his mother and was off. With one foot on the deck, he pushed hard with the other to get up steam. This pass was done in a crouch, with a leg straight out, the shift in his weight steering him through the cones; more subtle and more difficult.

Again and again he wove through the cones without knocking over a single one.

To an onlooker, he was just a boy showing off on a skateboard. To Linny this was a language better than words. He was giving his mother everything he had in him, a way of expressing what it was like to be a boy without his mother, to be left with rage and guilt and leftover love. He gave her the best he had in him, pouring his yearning and needy heart into his body's dance and putting it all at her service.

Two cars passed, hiding her from his view for a moment. Then he saw her.

Her white face was alight, smiling at him. It may have been the distance or a trick of shadow, but to his hungry gaze the sick and sour lines around her mouth and forehead were gone and Linny saw the face he knew before her bad heart had changed her. Killed her.

She leaned out and made a show of clapping. Then suddenly her head turned as if she had heard something. "Telephone," she mouthed.

While she was gone Linny planned his next moves in an ecstasy of triumph. That was nothing, he said to himself. Wait till she sees my ollie flip to backside grab. He looked to the lowering sky and hoped the rain would hold off until he was done.

When his mother returned to the window she made an agitated gesture for him to come to her. She was too upset to speak. He ran upstairs.

"That man!" she gasped. "Your Uncle Hal. He forgot. He's someplace out on Long Island. Tried to call Hilary but she's not home. Wants us to tell her. Sorry, he says. Will come right home. Take hours. Go, Linny. Right away. Find Hilary, poor child. Bring her here."

"I can't, Mom! I won't leave you!"

He couldn't bear the look she gave him. "You don't

understand," he cried. He couldn't believe this was happening. She was insisting that he leave her, and he dared not, vowed not. Not for an instant.

Memory of their last day together flooded him. But it was just the opposite then! Then she had pleaded with him to stay, and he had left her in anger—she, he, both of them angry. What hung in his memory was her face before he had slammed the door. It was that look, that terrible look he had thought was blame for him and he now knew with wrenching pity was plain fear. Fear of being alone. Fear of death.

He searched her face for some sign of it now, and there wasn't any. She wasn't afraid. Instead she was clear and intent, and the outrage on her face was worse than anger. It was all different this time! Maybe it would be all right.

He knelt by her chair and took her hand. "I'll go. I don't want to, but I'll go."

He looked down at the veined hand. "I have to tell you something, Mom. I have to." But now he found he didn't know what he wanted to say. There weren't words enough to tell what was in his muddled heart.

She leaned forward and said anxiously, "What? What is it?"

He blurted out, "I'm not mad at you, Mom. I don't want you to think that." With all their fights, the thought that she didn't know how he felt about her had haunted him for the whole year. And now that he had the chance to tell her, he couldn't.

Josie was able to smile at how serious he was. She shook her head at her son and said, "And that was the important thing you had to tell me? And here I thought you were going to tell me you were going to travel with the Olympics.

"Well now, you've been angry with me, Linny. Sure you have. It doesn't matter, don't you know that?" She stroked his hair, her fingers lingering on the black curls. "You've got a temper you have to watch, and I'm not easy. Don't you think I know how hard this has been for you? So come give me a kiss and don't worry about me. Now go get your cousin."

He stood. She said to him, "Linny?"

"Yes, Ma?"

"Have I ever told you you're my favorite son?"

"But Mom, I'm your only son!"

Her thin hand went to her forehead. "Oh," she said, deadpan. "No wonder."

There was one more thing Linny had to do before searching for Hilary. He took the ring from around his neck and let it dangle from the purple cord watching it swing and gleam for a sorry instant. Then he gave it to his mother to give to Eddie Gilberto in case he came by for it. A bet was a bet.

Linny pressed the ring in his mother's hand and went to find his abandoned cousin.

Chapter 17

Hilary sat forlorn and huddled against the door frame of her rowhouse. She barely glanced at Linny and went back to picking at a scab on her knee. She was still in her green linen dress for the outing with her father that afternoon, but now it was soiled and creased. The hemline looked as if she had blown her nose in it, which she had.

"Your father called," said Linny.

She was too busy with her knee to answer.

He sat on the step beside her and shook her to get her attention. "Did you hear what I said?"

She nodded but examined her scab as if it were the only thing in the world that interested her.

"Well, I'll tell you what he said even if you don't care. He tried to reach you, but I guess you were out here by then and didn't hear the phone. He's sorry, he was held up. He'll see you later." That was a lie. Uncle Hal had said that he had forgotten, but Linny spared her that.

This made Hilary smile grimly. "Yeah, sure." She looked up at the sky and closed her eyes over two tears that slid out from under them.

"Mom says to come on home with me, Hilly. Please, please hurry. You know I don't want to leave her alone today, and look where I am this minute!"

This roused Hilary a bit. "Oh no, this is the day! You go on home. Don't stay on my account. The contest over already?" She could barely muster up the interest.

"I couldn't go. Mom doesn't feel well, so I stayed home."

This drew once again the same grim smile. "What a pair of losers we are," she said. "Me with my father, and you, well, Aunt Josie, the tournament. Pathetic."

Linny was struck by that one. Her calling them pathetic was pathetic. He didn't feel that way at all. Not at that moment, he didn't. He was still too full of his performance on the skateboard before his audience of one, too near tears of gratitude for what felt to him very much like forgiveness. A stone had been lifted from his heart, and whatever else he could be called, loser wasn't it.

"What's so funny!" Hilary yelled at him, pushing him away. He hadn't known he was grinning.

"Hey, what are you mad at me for? Now come on, Hilly, get a move on. I'm in a hurry to get home. The day isn't over yet, remember? And anyway, you should know your father by now. Everybody else does. Let's go!"

" 'Everybody,' hey? Everybody but me." She stood and stretched. "Wait just a sec. I've got to get out of these stupid clothes."

By the time she returned, wearing her tank top and

158

shorts, it had begun to rain. She went back inside to get her poncho.

Hilary raised her head to the sky and was impressed. "Wow, will you look at that!"

Thick black clouds tinged with an eerie red had come boiling up out of nowhere, and were rolling toward them fast. The darkening sky was full of movement, gathering energy for the impending storm. Lightning flashed in the distance, followed soon after by a drumroll of thunder. The rain was still light, but the wind had risen, fluttering leaves and lifting trash.

The coming storm made Linny frantic to get home. He saw the dark threat of the sky and it struck his fearful heart that the elements were ganging up on him. This day, when death was to claim his mother, he wasn't the one to storm out of the house. This time the storm was outside of him, an overwhelming force that could keep him from her.

At that moment he wished he had the ring with him. He was ready to turn himself over to it. He needed help, and he had left it home with his mother.

"Let's take the bike," he said, putting on the poncho he had grabbed at home on the way out. "It's quicker."

Hilary sat on the handlebars and they set off. They were pedaling into the wind now and it was hard to make headway. This had a familiar feel to Linny, rain and wind buffeting them, Hilary on the handlebars. He quickly shut his mind to remembrance, not allowing it in. His fear gave him strength, and by straining he reached the corner and turned.

It was somewhat better around the corner. The worst

was over. When they turned the next corner the wind would be behind them and they could coast home. He breathed easier. Maybe he was wrong about the storm, maybe safety was near.

There was no letup. The rain was coming down heavier and the wind was picking up. The houses on both sides of the street acted as buffers and sheltered them from the worst of the wind, but it was heavy going.

"What is this?" yelled Hilary, who unlike Linny was exhilarated by the storm. It felt cleansing, washing her misery like a dirty rag.

The bike wobbled at a sudden gust and they jumped off so as not to crash. They were at a gate that led a few steps down to a basement apartment.

"Down here!" cried Hilary.

Linny bounced the bike down the steps to the small space in front of the door. They were protected from the wind and rain by an overhang.

Out of the wind it was suddenly quiet. Linny ran his hands over his hair, squeezing out water so it wouldn't drip into his eyes.

Hilly looked out into the weather but didn't see it. As if they were lolling on a beach blanket in the sun, instead of in the midst of a storm, she said to him, "You know what? Something must be wrong with me. My father? I see now what he does. I know it wasn't my mom who drove him away, I was just wanting it that way."

"Save it, Hilly. This is no time for that." He glared at the pelting rain as if it were a living enemy.

"No, listen, Linny, I know all about him now, and what I just realized is that it doesn't make any difference. You know what I mean? Is that crazy, or what?" She nodded to him as if he had answered, which he hadn't. He was peering out into the street trying to judge when to make a dash for it.

"Yeah," she said. She didn't know what to make of herself. She should hate her father. She did, she did! How could he do this to her, how could he be like that! So careless of people, so full of easy promises he didn't keep. No wonder her mother couldn't stand him, didn't want him, had divorced him.

And yet . . . Hilary thought of his big, burly presence, how he lit up a room, his laugh, how he could make her feel like a princess. Her perfect father, she had always thought. She wouldn't, couldn't, think of him in any other way.

But he wasn't perfect, and she knew that now. It was what followed that took her aback. She knew what he was like, and she found that she loved him anyway. He didn't have to be perfect for her to love. It was as if she had been looking at him through the binoculars he had once given her for her birthday. He was so large, so up close, that he had filled her whole vision. Now, without the binoculars, he was more the size of other people.

A clap of thunder that seemed to be directly overhead brought her back to the storm. Linny was afire to get home. If anything, it was raining even harder than when they had taken shelter, but he couldn't stay there any longer.

"Let's go!" he cried, seeing his mother in her chair where he had left her. He saw himself dash up the stairs. "Let her be there," he prayed.

Once again they cast off on the bike into the storm. Soaked and pummeled, they made it to Linny's corner, turned and let the wind carry them. It was at their backs now, pushing them so hard Linny didn't have to pedal. He held on to the handlebars as hard as he could and let the wind take them, thinking, Home, home, I'm almost there, I'm beating it, I'm going to keep her!

There was a great clap of thunder, and with it a giant fist of wind slapped them on the back and pushed them toward a tree. Linny saw it coming and had time in his mind to cry out his loss like a child—"Mama!"

Someone was holding him down. There was a hand on his chest holding him down. A voice in his ear said, "Okay, son, take it easy."

Linny let his eyes remain closed. The lids were much too heavy to open. He wanted to sink down again into the comfortable darkness, but his arm hurt him.

He heard the same voice whisper, "He's still under, poor kid, calling for his mother. Something you don't get over, isn't it. Helen, push that button, will you? Let's get the nurse in here."

Linny let them all go and sank down once again. What roused him was a slight sting on his cheek. This time a high, sharp voice said, "Wake up, Lionel. Let's see those Gypsy eyes."

Again a sting on his cheek. Someone was slapping his face. He opened his eyes to protest. Above him was a black saint with a white halo around her head.

He wanted to say, "Did I die? Are you an angel?" but they must have taken out his tongue and left him with

162

nothing but a stump. No tongue. He didn't care. Who needs it? He closed his eyes again.

"Open up, Lionel. You're doing just fine. We want you awake now." The saint with the halo had transformed herself into a nurse with round cheeks and gold-rimmed glasses. She turned her head away to say, "Sheriff? You wanted me to let you know when he was out of it. I'll give you five minutes."

Now bending over him was Sheriff Coleman. Linny recognized him. He smelled tobacco and wet wool. Something was dawning on Linny and he struggled to pin it down, but he didn't know what it was. Only that it was something terribly urgent.

"Wha . . . where?"

"You're here in the Colchester hospital, Linny, just coming out of surgery. Don't move around like that, son, you've got a broken arm there. Not to worry, you'll be batting out home runs again before you know it."

That would be nice. Linny had never hit a home run in his life, but maybe surgery had fixed that up for him.

The sheriff had something to ask him. "I don't want to disturb you, son, but you must know that you gave us quite a scare this afternoon. Now see if you can remember back. It's a bothersome thing to me. I tell you, I went over that ground time and time again looking for you kids. My men, your Aunt Helen, the Dilts, we went through those woods stone by stone. You were gone, just gone."

Sheriff Coleman shook his head in puzzlement, and his jowls waggled like a basset hound's.

Linny's Aunt Helen appeared and leaned over him. She kissed his forehead and cried, "Thank God! You have no idea!" To the sheriff she said, "Now Stan, that's enough. You go on home and let the boy be. Plenty of time for this later."

"All right, Helen. He's asleep again, anyway. Main thing is, we found 'em. Though how we could go over and over the same ground and not see them, I'll never know." As if to himself he mused, "And then there they were, plain as day." He stopped to breathe in and out a few times. "Say so long to the boy for me."

Linny had closed his eyes. He heard the footsteps recede and then the door close. He managed to ask, "Hilly?"

"Next room," said Aunt Helen. "Taylor's with her now. They tell me it's a concussion. She'll be all right, my baby. She'll get her memory back. But I tell you, Linny . . ." She pressed a handkerchief to her lips and couldn't continue.

The shock for his aunt must have been great and gone deep since he had never heard her take so little time to say so much. Maybe, like him with his baseball, she was about to acquire a new skill.

No, she wasn't. Aunt Helen kept going. "I'll never, never forget it, as long as I live. There it was, getting dark, all of us with our flashlights, terrified out of our wits. The road gone, everything underwater on the other side, and maybe you in it. And then that blessed shout of Taylor's: 'Found them!' Never, never," she cried into her handkerchief, "never."

She looked up. "Why did I let you go this morning!" She buried her face again. Looked up. "Your father is

164

going to have a thing or two to say when he hears this. Lucky I can't get hold of him."

Memory flooded Linny. A strangled cry escaped him. He thrashed his head from side to side to rid himself of where he was. So real, so real! Just minutes ago he and Hilary were in a storm headed home to his mother. They had been back to before all the bad things had happened. And now here they were again at the barn. The bad things had already happened.

"No, no," he shouted silently, or so he thought.

"Nurse!"

"I'll thank you to leave us now, Mrs. Brier. Your daughter is asking for you."

Linny was given an injection, and he sank down gratefully into the friendly dark once more.

He awoke some time later. His room was dark except for a night light over the door. Outside in the hospital corridor all was quiet, except for occasional footsteps. Visiting hours were long over.

He remembered everything. Hilary was next door. He had to see her!

By his door was a wheelchair. That was his first goal. He would have to get himself to it somehow. His head was clear, but the cast on his arm made it awkward for him to maneuver. Holding onto the rail of the bed, he took a few steps, wishing he had his skateboard under him instead of wobbly feet. If he fell now, he'd need a body cast.

He reached the wheelchair, managed to get the door open and peered out. At the end of the corridor was the nurses' station. Two nurses were talking. He could hear their hushed voices. One of them faced him but was absorbed in her conversation. Somewhere he could hear a child crying. A hospital at night was creepy, he decided.

Linny had to wait until the nurses went about their business. They separated and entered rooms down the hall. The coast was clear.

He quickly wheeled himself to the room next door, in a sweaty hope that it was the right one.

It was. The light was on at Hilary's bedside. From the doorway she looked as pale as the bandage wrapped around her head. He wheeled himself to her bedside and sighed to himself, Oh, Hilly. She was the only one in the world who knew, the only one he wanted to talk to.

Her eyes were closed. "Hilly?" he said softly, waiting for her look of amazement at what had happened to them, at where they were.

She awoke and opened big eyes to him. He leaned forward in the wheelchair and wondered if she would be glad or sorry they were back.

What she said was, "I didn't vomit once this morning."

Linny stared at her blankly.

She said, "Taylor says you broke your arm. I broke my head and you broke your arm. Pretty funny, I say."

Linny blinked at her, not knowing where to start. In a hoarse whisper he cried, "Hilly, Hilly, what's the matter with you? We're back! We were headed for a tree, and bang, no more glitch, no more last year. Here we are back in our own time. Don't you remember?"

She drew away from him in the bed and whimpered. "You're talking crazy, Linny, you're scaring me."

"Please, Hilly. Keep your voice down. I'm not sup-posed to be here. It happened! I couldn't have dreamed it up. We were on the bike looking around at the flood and then we were back a year. Back to before Mom died and before Uncle Hal left. Remember Walt and the Wightman twins?"

Hilary kept staring at him and shaking her head.

"What about the ring? And what about Uncle Hal? Don't you remember your father?"

This last caused a flicker, a change from utter blank-ness. Cautiously she said to him, "I remember the flood all right, and riding around looking at it. You know, when you said that just now, I mean said about remembering my father, I had this funny feeling."

"Yeah! That's it! What about the feeling?"

She drew the sheet higher. "Oh, I don't know what it was. It's gone now." She added, with a smooth accepting face, "I'll be getting a postcard pretty soon, I guess. Oh, well."

She sighed and slid farther down in the bed. "I have this headache. Taylor says I got a real bang on the head when we totaled the bike. You know, I don't remember that at all. Weird, huh?"

She was drifting off when some thought roused her. "The ring. I remember it now. It's coming back."

A fervent hope sprang up in Linny. He leaned forward.

"We found a ring in that old abandoned house. We went exploring and I found it. I was wearing it." Hilary felt around her neck. "Where is it?"

Out of his helpless confusion, the only answer Linny could give her was the simple truth as he knew it. "I gave it to my mom to give to Eddie Gilberto. I owed it to him."

Hilary looked at him funny and closed her eyes again. "Big joke. I'm supposed to be the one who tells stories," she murmured.

He was exhausted and wanted to get back to his bed so he could bury himself under the covers. He had heard that you could have outlandish dreams when you were under anesthesia. He had hit a tree, so okay, maybe it was that.

Hilary was asleep and he felt entirely alone. He looked about the shadowed room. How suddenly small it was, small and practical, with equipment on the trays and walls and behind the bed to hold you to everyday life. He was overcome by his own foolishness. Of course there was some ordinary explanation, accident or anesthesia. How in the world could it be otherwise?

"Mom?" he tested, waiting for the ghost in his head to have her say, to scold him. Nothing. Gone. No ghost.

As he thought of his mother a welling of pure grief overcame him. He put his head back and closed his eyes to let the tears slide down his cheeks in a noiseless and final good-bye. Whatever he had been through, dream or accident, the thought of his mother was different. It left him sad and yearning, but without the old hurtful blame to squeeze his heart.

Footsteps. The door opened and a flabbergasted nurse stood over him. "Why, young man, what on earth are you doing here!" It wasn't a question. She pushed him out the door and back to his room.

"Into that bed!" she ordered. He let her help him

gratefully. When he was tucked in safely under his sheet, she said, "You can see your cousin in the morning. She had a nasty knock same as you, so don't you be wandering in there again until we say so."

She pulled an envelope from the pocket of her uniform and said, "I came in here to put this on your tray for the morning. One of your visitors told me to give it to you. Name of Taylor Dilt. He said for me to tell you that he found the contents on the ground underneath you. Is it yours, he wants to know. Would you like to look at it now or wait till morning?"

"Now, please."

Linny shook the contents onto his outstretched palm. Round and gleaming and true as hope was the ring.

He shook the envelope again, and into his hand fell bits of dirt and leaves. Mixed with these traces were some purple threads.

The nurse clucked, "Well, will you look at that. I heard the yarn factory had left bits of color all along the river after the flood. You've got some there. Now off to sleep with you." She turned out his light.

But Linny knew what he had seen! Taylor had lifted the ring and bits of what had clung to it. The threads were from the purple cord his mother had tied on the ring for Hilary two days before. They must be. He willed it so.

He put the envelope under his pillow. Outside the window he saw the full moon make silver the mountains in the near distance. The moon was so bright that from his bed he thought he could make out the ski trails that parted the trees like a comb.

He saw himself on his skateboard, streaking down the trails. He took off, up and away. He was in the air, skimming the currents, skating across the face of the moon, balanced perfectly. He was flying, and it was easy, for he was living in a world where anything was possible.

/FIC.SL275BA>Cl/

FIC. SL275BA
Slepian, Jan.
Back to before

Rosary College Library
River Forest, Illinois